Once upon a time, there lived a prince who could not find a bride. Fearing the family line would end, the prince's mother gave him an enchanted ring that would fit only his one true love. Maidens traveled from near and far to try on the ring, but to no avail. Then, one day, the daughter of a visiting merchant slipped the ring onto her finger—a perfect fit. Upon the royal wedding, the prince fell in love with his princess bride, and his marriage thrived. Untold prosperity, happiness and peace befell the citizens of his country. And all lived happily ever after.

As the years passed, the legend of the royal engagement ring evolved and became tradition. To this day, if the ruling or crown prince has not wed by his thirtieth year, unwed females of marriageable age are encouraged to try on the ring. If the ring fits, within seven days the prince must marry the woman wearing it, or abdicate the throne.

And our story begins...

Dear Reader,

Not only is February the month for lovers, it is the second month for readers to enjoy exciting celebratory titles across all Silhouette series. Throughout 2000, Silhouette Books will be commemorating twenty years of publishing the best in contemporary category romance fiction. This month's Silhouette Romance lineup continues our winning tradition.

Carla Cassidy offers an emotional VIRGIN BRIDES title, in which a baby on the doorstep sparks a second chance for a couple who'd once been *Waiting for the Wedding*—their own!—and might be again.... Susan Meier's charming miniseries BREWSTER BABY BOOM continues with *Bringing Up Babies*, as black sheep brother Chas Brewster finds himself falling for the young nanny hired to tend his triplet half siblings.

A beautiful horse trainer's quest for her roots leads her to two men in Moyra Tarling's *The Family Diamond. Simon Says... Marry Me!* is the premiere of Myrna Mackenzie's THE WEDDING AUCTION. Don't miss a single story in this engaging three-book miniseries. A pregnant bride-for-hire dreams of making *The Double Heart Ranch* a real home, but first she must convince her husband in this heart-tugger by Leanna Wilson. And *If the Ring Fits...* some lucky woman gets to marry a prince! In this sparkling debut Romance from Melissa McClone, an accident-prone American heiress finds herself a royal bride-to-be!

In coming months, look for Diana Palmer, a Joan Hohl-Kasey Michaels duet and much more. It's an exciting year for Silhouette Books, and we invite you to join the celebration!

Happy Reading!

Mary-Theresa Hussey

Mary-Theresa Hussey
Senior Editor

Please address questions and book requests to:
Silhouette Reader Service
U.S.: 3010 Walden Ave., P.O. Box 1325, Buffalo, NY 14269
Canadian: P.O. Box 609, Fort Erie, Ont. L2A 5X3

IF THE RING FITS...

Melissa McClone

Silhouette
ROMANCE™
Published by Silhouette Books
America's Publisher of Contemporary Romance

To Mary-Theresa Hussey,
for planting the seed and letting it grow.

Special thanks to Monica and Shirley for all their help
and Mike Weis for sharing Francis.

 SILHOUETTE BOOKS

ISBN 0-373-19431-5

IF THE RING FITS...

Copyright © 2000 by Melissa Martinez McClone

Visit us at www.romance.net

Printed in U.S.A.

Books by Melissa McClone

Silhouette Romance

If the Ring Fits... #1431

Silhouette Yours Truly

Fiancé for the Night

MELISSA McCLONE

With a degree in mechanical engineering from Stanford University, the last thing Melissa McClone ever thought she would be doing is writing romance novels, but analyzing engines for a major U.S. airline just couldn't compete with her "happily-ever-afters."

When she isn't writing, caring for her toddler or doing laundry, Melissa loves to curl up on the couch with a cup of tea, her cats and a good book. She is also a big fan of *The X-Files* and enjoys watching home decorating shows to get ideas for her house—a 1939 cottage that is *slowly* being renovated.

Melissa lives in Lake Oswego, Oregon, with her own real-life hero husband, daughter, two lovable, but oh-so-spoiled indoor cats and a no-longer-stray outdoor kitty who decided to call the garage home. Melissa loves to hear from readers. You can write to her at P.O. Box 63, Lake Oswego, OR 97034.

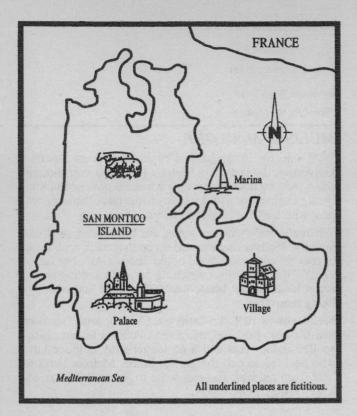

FRANCE

N

Marina

SAN MONTICO
ISLAND

Palace

Village

Mediterranean Sea

All underlined places are fictitious.

Chapter One

"Did you know she set fire to the White House, Your Highness?" Didier Alois whispered.

His Serene Highness Prince Richard de Thierry of San Montico stared at the unlikely pyromaniac—a young woman with a heart-shaped face and striking emerald eyes that matched her gown. The fitted bodice accentuated her cleavage and small waist. Her curly auburn hair flowed like silk past her shoulders and glimmered beneath the light of the crystal chandelier. Making her way along the Great Hall and the slow-moving receiving line, she curtsied and flashed a dazzling smile at dignitaries and royalty.

"Who is she?"

"Christina Armstrong, Your Highness," Didier answered, loud enough to be heard above the din of the guests, but soft enough to be heard only by Richard.

Trust Didi to know everything about the guests attending the royal birthday ball. Then again, as royal advisor that was his job.

Richard wondered what else his best friend knew about

Christina Armstrong. He was certain they had never met, but something about her seemed familiar. He noticed the older gentleman escorting her. And then it hit Richard. "Armstrong? As in Alan Armstrong, billionaire CEO and patriarch of America's second most famous family?"

"Yes, Your Highness."

Richard knew the type—he had been engaged to one—a rich man's daughter who still used her daddy's titanium card. Wealthy, spoiled, a title-seeking princess wanna-be.

He clenched his gloved hands. "I told my mother not to invite any Americans. You know how they are about... royalty."

"I doubt your mother had a choice but to invite them, considering the substantial donation Armstrong International made to her charity fund." Didier hesitated. "Not all American women are like—"

"This has nothing to do with her." *Nothing at all.* But the way Richard's chest tightened told him it did. Regaining control, he lowered his voice. "This is my birthday. I should have been consulted about the guest list."

"Judging from the quality of the women who have arrived, I believe Princess Marguerite did quite well without your input, Your Highness." Didier smiled. "I must say, Christina Armstrong even looks like a princess. She's quite lovely. And with her upbringing and connections—"

"She is nothing more than an American heiress."

"The legend cares nothing about—"

"The legend, Didi?" Simply saying the word "legend" put a bitter taste in Richard's mouth. "Do you truly believe the royal engagement ring is going to fit one of these women, that we will find true love and everlasting happiness, that the island will prosper with our marriage?"

"I do, Your Highness."

Ridiculous, utterly ridiculous. Even logical Didier believed in the Legend of the Ring, in magic. But Richard knew better. The pursuit of true love—any kind of love—brought only heartache. Magic did not exist. Yet duty to his family and his country bound him to the legend. If only he had married…

Strains of Vivaldi, played by the seventy-piece orchestra, drifted in from the ballroom. They might as well play a requiem for all the fun Richard would have tonight. He knew what to expect, and he dreaded it.

Women, dressed in designer gowns, dreamed of trying on the ring and having it fit. Men, wearing tuxedos, waited to console those it did not fit. The air kissing, the meaningless toasts, the inconsequential conversations. His so-called guests had less substance than the effervescent bubbles rising in the overpriced champagne his mother had ordered.

He should never have agreed to this farce of a party. Never. He should be sailing, relaxing on his yacht and drinking his favorite beer. If it were not for the legend…

The Legend.

Richard wanted no part of it. He didn't believe in the legend any more than he believed in the tooth fairy or love at first sight. Perhaps a hundred years ago, legends made some sort of sense, but not today.

He was following his father's wish and bringing San Montico into the present, but it was a monumentally slow task. Each step toward progress was a battle against the majority who resisted change. The harder Richard pushed for progress, the harder the people fought against it. The citizens of the island clung to old-fashioned traditions and myths like drowning rats on lifelines during a raging storm at sea.

It had not taken Richard long to realize the antiquated customs, such as the Legend of the Ring, that people held so dear to their hearts prevented San Montico from moving forward. Only by doing away with the old ways could real progress take place. Once Richard proved the legend was nothing more than a fairy tale, San Montico could take a giant leap toward modernization. It was the best thing for his country, the best thing for himself.

"The legend is pure fantasy, Didi, and I will prove it. As soon as the clock strikes midnight, this will be over."

"Perhaps it will be only the beginning. The legend has proved itself true in the past, Your Highness."

Richard would not believe it. "It is nothing more than a self-fulfilling prophecy. The legend came true because my ancestors, including my own parents, chose to make it come true. I choose not to. Why don't you get married and take the pressure off me?"

Didier sighed. "If you recall, Your Highness, tradition dictates I not marry until you do."

Another stupid custom. Richard's marital status should have nothing to do with his royal advisor's. If only Didier wasn't so entrenched in following the "old" ways. "I should have known there was another reason for you to want me to marry."

"My only reason has to do with our country. You need to find a wife, Your Highness."

"I have tried to find a wife, Didi." Richard had done everything possible not to fall prey to the legend. He had dated more than his share of women. Up until six months ago, he thought he had found *the one,* only to be hugely mistaken. Since then, it had been a race to find another. But he could not open up his heart to just anyone. "I've gone above and beyond the call of duty. Surely that must count."

"But none of your efforts has...succeeded, Your Highness. You are still unmarried, and San Montico needs an heir."

Richard was tired of hearing what San Montico expected of him. He knew. It had been drummed into him from the day he was born. He straightened his gloves. "I can provide an heir without marrying."

Didier cringed. "Your Highness."

Perhaps Richard had overstepped the boundary with that one, but he couldn't help himself. No one was on his side. The entire island, including his mother and uncle, expected him to fall in love and marry one of the women attending his birthday ball. "Look at the problems other royal families have had, especially the Windsors. An arranged marriage simply to provide an heir makes no sense and adds nothing but more stress to an outdated institution."

"Are you talking about matrimony or monarchies, Your Highness?"

Leave it to Didier to make Richard laugh.

"We will have to finish this discussion later," Didier whispered. "Here comes Mr. Armstrong and his daughter, Your Highness."

Richard nodded.

The dignified, tuxedo-clad Alan Armstrong bowed in front of him. "Your Highness, may I present my daughter, Christina."

Attractive, yes. Princess material, no. Her rosy blush and wide eyes told Richard she was impressed by him, probably even in awe of him. What more could he expect from an American? When he married, he would select a woman who saw him as a man, not a prince. In the meantime, he forced a smile. "It is my pleasure to meet your lovely daughter."

She curtsied. "Happy birthday, Your Gorgeous, I mean, Your *Highness*."

Richard refrained from rolling his eyes. "Thank you, Miss Armstrong." He raised her trembling hand to his mouth and kissed it. Her skin felt soft and warm beneath his lips. He caught the faint scent of cocoa butter on her honeyed-tan skin. Had she sunbathed topless at the beach today? "I am delighted you could come."

As he released her hand, she dropped her beaded clutch bag. Bending over, he reached for it. So did Christina and thwacked her head against his forehead. Jerking away, she stumbled, but her father's quick action saved her from falling onto the marble floor.

"I'm so sorry." She touched Richard's arm—a breach in royal protocol—and he stiffened. "Are you okay, Your Highness?"

The sooner he got rid of her, the better. Ignoring the throbbing pain in his head, Richard handed her the bag. "I am fine."

Before Christina could say or do anything else, her father pushed her toward the end of the receiving line. "Your Highness, my wife sends her regrets for missing your birthday ball, but she had a prior engagement."

As Richard nodded, he caught a glimpse of Christina walking toward the ballroom and watched the sway of her gown. Her image blurred slightly as if she were an angel surrounded by clouds. An angel, she wasn't. He must have hit his head harder than he realized. Richard rubbed his forehead, and she glanced back at him. Their gazes locked for an instant. At the same time, she reached forward to shake the extended hand of...

No.

Fighting the urge to cry out, Richard gritted his teeth. Christina shook the hand, not of a man, but a suit of armor. One of the chain mail gloves came off, leaving the priceless antiquity handless.

Damn. Not even the bloodiest of battles fought preserving San Montico from French and Spanish invaders had destroyed the armor, but this woman, this American... His muscles tightened; his blood pressure soared. Add another headache to his already aching forehead. Christina stared at the glove in horror, then tried to hide it behind her small purse. Alan Armstrong muttered what sounded like a well-rehearsed apology.

Richard accepted the apology with an obligatory smile. Now was not the time to show emotion. Not with the palace full of guests. He would remain calm, impassive. It was only a glove, a glove that had belonged to his family for ages. He stared at Christina. "Do you need assistance, Miss Armstrong?"

She raised the glove and grinned. "I seem to have found an extra hand already."

At least she had a sense of humor. And she had not set the palace on fire. Yet. Richard breathed a sigh of relief. "One can never have too many hands."

Her eyes sparkled. "What should I do with, uh, this?"

"Didier," Richard said, "please assist Miss Armstrong."

"Yes, Your Highness." Didier stepped away from him and took the glove from her. "I'm sorry for any inconvenience."

"I'm sorry for breaking it," Christina said.

"You didn't break it," Didier said before Richard could answer. "It's…old."

Just like all the other irreplaceable works of art in the palace. Richard had been warned about her setting fire to the White House. He would not allow the same nonsense to happen here—the legend was nonsense enough. He would make sure someone kept Christina Armstrong away from any open flames. It was going to be a long enough night without any unexpected pyrotechnics.

Armstrongs are never impressed. Armstrongs are never impressed. The mantra of her snobbish family echoed in her mind. Christina had always had a difficult time remembering not to be impressed, but tonight it was impossible.

It was all she could do not to stare, openmouthed. Her family was obscenely wealthy—and often flaunted the fact—but this... She had never seen such a tasteful display of riches. Exquisite antiques, famous paintings by the masters, breathtaking chandeliers and tantalizing buffets of gourmet cuisine filled each of the public rooms at the fairytale-worthy San Montico palace. But none of those wonderful treasures came close to the beauty of the prince himself.

Simply a glimpse of him made her pulse quicken. Bells chimed and the sound hung in the festive air, but Christina realized it was only the clinking of crystal champagne flutes.

Exuding an aura of charm that drew people in like a tractor beam, Prince Richard spoke with a small group of women who hung on his every word. Christina stood a polite distance away. She wanted to memorize everything about him so she could sketch a drawing when she returned to her hotel room.

He was Prince Charming in the flesh. Nothing, including the elaborate tapestry that hung on the wall behind him or the sparkling jewels the women wore, could compare to Prince Richard in his white uniform with shiny gold trim and royal-blue sash. The romantic melody played by a harpist in the corner echoed her sentiments.

Prince Richard smiled, and Christina drew in a sharp breath. No man deserved to be that good-looking. Sinfully sexy. That was the only way to describe him. Over six feet tall, he carried himself with a regal air. His aristocratic nose, high cheekbones and chiseled features were softened by his full lips, to-die-for lush lashes and a boyish dimple on his left cheek that appeared every so often when he smiled. The contrast—devastating. With eyes the color of the water surrounding the island of Santorini and thick, sun-bleached wavy hair, the prince had been dubbed the catch of the decade.

Catch of the century was a better title.

Too bad he was a prince whose every move was followed by the rabid press, the inquisitive public and his adoring fans. Not that she cared tonight. It was too magical an evening to let the thought of publicity ruin anything. Not even the paparazzi dared make an appearance here. She could be Cinderella at the prince's ball and not worry about appearing in the tabloids for one night. She could forget about life's harsh realities until tomorrow.

Christina glanced up at the well-preserved frescoes painted on the ceiling. She could almost smell the layers of lime plaster and pigment, the sweat of the painter who created it years, maybe centuries, ago. A delightful cherub smiled down at her, and Christina didn't feel so all alone.

"Are you having a good time, Miss Armstrong?"

The voice came from behind her. Turning, she saw the prince's assistant standing behind a table. His smile betrayed nothing, but he must have seen her staring at the prince like a lovesick puppy dog. The fact she wasn't the only one doing so saved her from total embarrassment. She straightened her posture. "Yes, I am."

"I am Didier Alois, royal advisor to the prince. We met earlier."

Remembering the incident with the armor, she chuckled. It wasn't quite the impression she wanted to make. "Yes, we did."

He motioned to his right. "Have you tried on the ring?"

"No, I haven't." The ring sat on a small pedestal covered with black velvet. If she hadn't been so busy making goo-goo eyes at the prince, she would have noticed it immediately. "What is it?"

"It's the royal engagement ring." Didier removed the ring from the platform. Multicolored light was reflected off the different facets cut on the center stone, a diamond. "All the de Thierry brides have worn it."

As beautiful as any of the crown jewels on display at the Tower of London, the large diamond glimmered under the overhead lights. The ring was almost medieval-looking with a wide filigree gold band inlaid with rubies, emeralds and sapphires. "It's breathtaking."

"Please, try it on."

"I don't think that's a good idea."

"But you must," Didier said. "All the women at the ball are required to try on the ring. Prince Richard will be upset if you don't."

Christina didn't want to upset the prince, but she didn't want to cause another incident, either. Apart from the chain mail glove, she'd managed to stay out of trouble. No sense pushing her luck. She took a step backward.

"Please, Miss Armstrong," Didier coaxed. "We must see if it fits."

"If the ring fits, do I win a prize or something?"

Didier grinned. "Or something."

Christina glanced back at the prince. It would be nice to try on the ring, his ring. A chance of a lifetime. A chance to really be Cinderella at the ball. And how could she get in trouble if the prince's own advisor had told her to try it on? Not even her father could get upset about it. The ring was way too small anyway. No way would it fit. After a moment of hesitation, she extended her left hand. "Okay."

Didier brought the ring to her finger. Funny, but it almost felt like heat was emanating from the gold band. Must be Didier. Men were always hot. When the ring touched her skin, a buzz of electricity shot up her arm. She gasped, but Didier continued sliding the ring onto her finger. When he let go of her hand, Christina couldn't believe it. The ring fit.

She stared at it. Beautiful. Someday, she would have an

engagement ring of her own. Not this spectacular. A simple gold band would do. All she wanted was to find a man who would love her for who she was, a man who wanted what she did—children, pets, a porch with a swing. A normal life, a normal family.

No more limelight. No more photographs or headlines or snide remarks in gossip columns. No more twelve-inch-thick prenuptial agreements to protect an inheritance she didn't want.

Didier furrowed his brow. "Are you all right, miss?"

"Yes," Christina said, feeling warm and a little dizzy. Too much sun, too much champagne, too much lusting after Prince Richard. The proverbial clock had struck midnight. Time for this Cinderella to call it a night. "Thank you for letting me try it on. It's exquisite."

She pulled on the ring, but it wouldn't budge.

Didier leaned toward her. "Is there a problem, Miss Armstrong?"

Christina pulled on it again, but her fingertips simply slid over the elaborately decorated band. The ring wouldn't even twirl around her finger. "It seems to be stuck."

"Let me try, miss." Didier straightened his shoulders and tugged on the ring until Christina cried out in pain. "It doesn't seem to be moving."

She couldn't understand why Didier smiled as if he'd just won the lottery. "I must get this ring off. If my father finds out, he'll kill me. And the prince..." A glance told her Prince Richard was too engrossed in his conversation to realize what was happening. Christina wanted to keep it that way. "Would it be okay if I went to the ladies' room and tried to remove it?"

For some reason, Didier seemed to be enjoying himself. His brown eyes twinkled; his smile grew wider. He looked almost giddy. "I don't think it's coming off."

"Please." Why had she allowed this to happen? She knew better. "I'd like to try."

From his peripheral vision, Richard saw Didier approach. It was about time. If Richard heard one more boring piece of gossip about the United Kingdom's royal family, he was going to reinstate flogging.

"May I speak with you for a moment, Your Highness?" Didier asked.

"Of course." Richard bowed to the women surrounding him. "Excuse me, ladies." As soon as the women were out of earshot, he sighed. "Thank you for coming to my aid, Didi. I never thought I would escape with all my clothes on. I felt like a rabbit surrounded by panting wolves. I was hoping you would leave the ring long enough to rescue me." Richard glanced at its pedestal, the empty pedestal. No guard. No ring. His stomach knotted. "Where is the ring?"

Didier's wide grin answered his question.

No. This could not be happening.

The legend wasn't true; it wasn't. The legend dictated he had to marry the woman whom the ring fit within a week or abdicate. He would do neither.

It was his duty to marry and produce an heir. He would, but not because he was turning thirty and a legend dictated it. He would marry *whom* he wanted, *when* he wanted.

Every decision in his life had been made for the sake of San Montico. He had sacrificed childhood dreams and adult desires for his family, his people, his country. But the choice of a wife was his, and his alone, to make. "Does anyone know? My mother?"

"No, we can make an announce—"

"Tell no one." Richard needed time to think, time to come up with a plan. He would not let San Montico's sentimental attachment to a legend take away the most important choice of his life and keep him from modernizing the country. "Where is…it?"

"In the ladies' lounge," Didier said. "With Miss Armstrong."

Not her. Please not her.

"May I suggest a course of action, Your Highness?"

Richard clenched his teeth. "No. You have done enough."

Please work. Please. Christina lathered her hands with soap. But the ring wouldn't budge, not a fraction of an inch, not even a millimeter. She rinsed her hands, double-checking the drain plug on the gold-plated sink. Not that a ring this size could fit, but she wasn't taking any chances.

Staring at the ring on her red, swollen finger, Christina fought the urge to scream. She could have said no when her mother insisted she come to San Montico, but accepting the invitation had seemed like such a little thing to make her mother happy. Only now…

Christina would disappoint her parents. Again. She should have known no matter how hard she tried, she would never be able to please them. But no, she'd gone against her better judgment and said yes. And embarrassed herself. Her family. Her country. Wait until her mother found out.

What if the ring didn't come off? Christina flexed her hand. Surely they wouldn't want to chop her finger off? She was an artist. She needed all her fingers. Time to give the soap another try.

Perhaps she was overreacting a little, but this was a small island in the Mediterranean ruled by a prince, not the U.S. government. San Montico might never have heard of due process of law. They might even follow another law—an eye for an eye, a hand for a hand. She lathered again.

Maybe her father could do something—open a factory,

build a resort, pay off the national debt. Maybe the prince would understand. Maybe her life was over.

She added more soap, but the ring still wouldn't budge.

As her stomach curled up and turned one somersault after another, she leaned against the marble counter and groaned. "What am I going to do?"

A man cleared his throat. "Excuse me."

In the mirror, Christina saw Prince Richard's reflection. He stood with his arms folded across his chest and an unreadable expression on his face. He looked more like a pirate than a prince. A mean pirate. So much for him understanding.

"I knocked, but no one answered."

Turning, Christina didn't know what to say. His wide shoulders and six-foot-plus height made the bathroom seem smaller. "Your Highness, I—"

Didier walked into the bathroom, smiling. "The ring fits, Your Highness."

Prince Richard's nostrils flared. His full lips nearly disappeared as his mouth tightened. Angry, oh boy, was he angry. How was she going to get out of this one?

"I wouldn't say it fits, Your Highness." Christina hoped she wouldn't cause another international incident. "It's stuck. I'm probably retaining water. You know, PMS and all that stuff."

"No, Miss Armstrong." Prince Richard cocked an eyebrow. "I would not know."

Why did she say that? He was a prince. She was an Armstrong. Heat rose in her cheeks. "Of course, you wouldn't. I'm—"

"Let me see your hand."

She showed him her soap-covered hand. "Maybe if I try some lotion or—"

"Quiet."

The harsh tone of his voice silenced her. Christina swallowed hard. Prince Charming had disappeared. The classical lines of his face now seemed hard, not handsome. The set of his chin now seemed arrogant, not confident. If only she could turn back the clock and return to the ball...

Prince Richard removed his gloves. He pulled on the ring until tears welled in her eyes. She bit her tongue to keep from crying out.

"It fits, Your Highness," Didier said with a smile.

"It does not fit." The prince washed and dried his hands. "It is stuck, Didi. It is too small, that is all."

"The legend says—"

"Wash your hands, Miss Armstrong," he ordered before Didier could say another word.

"What legend?" Christina asked.

"Wash your hands," the prince ordered. "I will not ask again."

"Yes, Your Highness," Christina mumbled, feeling like a newly enlisted marine in boot camp. She scrubbed but couldn't rinse all the soap out of the filigree band.

"Find Mr. Armstrong," Prince Richard commanded. "I need to speak with him immediately."

"Your Highness." Didier stopped at the door. "Perhaps—"

"Not now, Didi." As soon as the door closed behind Didier, Prince Richard handed her his white gloves. "Put these on."

The left glove was at least two sizes too big. "It doesn't fit, Your Highness."

"This is not a fashion show, Miss Armstrong. You will wear them. I do not need to have my mother see you wearing the ring. Or the press."

The press. Prince Richard had a good point. She put on the right glove.

He walked toward the door. "Come with me."

Uncertain and a little frightened, Christina hesitated.

"Now."

She tilted her chin, trying to gain a bit of courage. "Where are we going, Your Highness?"

"Some place private, where we will not be disturbed."

The palace reminded her of a dream castle, but the evening was turning into a nightmare. Surely the palace didn't have a dungeon with a torture chamber. She followed Prince Richard out of the bathroom to a narrow, dimly lit hallway. "Exactly where is that, Your Highness?"

"My bedroom."

Chapter Two

Christina stood outside the double white-paneled doors, her heart pounding in her throat. The prince, the engagement ring, his bedroom.

Oh, man. His bedroom, the prince's bedroom.

No one would believe this was happening. Well, maybe her family would, but no one else. She pinched her arm to make sure she wasn't dreaming.

Prince Richard stepped in front of her and opened one of the doors. "You will wait inside."

"Your Highness," she said, then hesitated.

His I'm-better-than-you stare made her feel unwelcome, emphasizing the fact she didn't belong. "What is it, Miss Armstrong?"

Christina might not be royalty, but she was an Armstrong. She forced herself to look him straight in the eye. "I'm sorry for ruining your birthday."

"Go on." With his hand at the small of her back, he led her inside. It was obvious he could care less about her apology. "Do not touch anything and stay away from the windows."

She almost asked if she should remove her shoes before stepping on the carpet but thought better of it. "Yes, Your Highness."

"I must return to the party. I believe my uncle is going to have a heart attack."

A what? Heart attack? She tried to speak, but no words would come. Prince Richard closed the door behind her, and she heard a click. Christina tried the handle, but it was locked.

Locked in the prince's bedroom. Alone.

But a heart attack? Was Prince Richard joking or did he really mean... She glanced at her gloved hand.

The ring. It had to be the ring.

Oh, no. What had she done? A heart attack. This was her worst yet. People died from heart attacks. Christina clutched her hands to her chest. She'd really done it this time. The marquess—such a charming, entertaining man. Unlike his nephew, Prince Richard.

A heart attack.

Awful, dreadful, inexcusable.

What would her family—make that the world—think? For once, she would deserve everything the press threw at her. She truly would not deserve to be an Armstrong.

She plopped onto the king-size bed, a fit-for-a-prince bed made of elegantly carved mahogany with pomegranate-shaped finials on the canopy posts. Through an open window, a gentle breeze, carrying the smell of the sea, filled the room, but the fresh air did nothing to ease the suffocating guilt.

Her fault.

Lying on the hard mattress, Christina pulled the gloves up to keep them from falling off. Over the years, she'd broken things, valuable things. She'd started a war, actually a small insurrection, as her father preferred to call it. But she'd never hurt...

Okay, that wasn't exactly true. But breaking Tom's thumb with the winch handle during a regatta could have happened to anyone. And Ron's concussion was a total accident. Grabbing that cast-iron skillet was instinct, pure and simple. He could have been a burglar. If only she'd seen the box of Ho Hos first, but no one drops by at midnight unannounced. No one but Ron. At least she hadn't had a gun. The gun, she couldn't forget about Kent. But that was his fault, one hundred percent. Kent knew better than to take her skeet shooting. Thank goodness for the advances in medical technology. It was amazing what could be surgically reattached.

Okay, so she might have *accidentally* hurt a few men, but she'd never killed anyone. A heart attack? Tears welled in her eyes. The stupid ring. She'd cut off her finger if it would save the marquess. She really would. She'd do anything to rid herself of the helpless feeling settling in the pit of her stomach like a week old glazed doughnut.

After what seemed like a forever of silence, the lock on the door clicked. As Christina sat up, one of the double doors opened. Prince Richard stepped inside, followed by Didier and the marquess.

The marquess.

Thank goodness. He wasn't dead. Christina ran and wrapped her arms around him. "You're alive."

The marquess smiled. "Now more than ever."

She stared into his twinkling blue eyes, eyes that reminded her of the prince. Or *had* until she saw the real man beneath the princely facade. "I thought I'd killed you."

"My dear Christina. May I call you that?"

Nodding, she couldn't stop looking at the marquess. He was alive. Alive. A warm tear slipped down her cheek.

"Are those tears for me?" The marquess wiped her cheek with a white linen handkerchief. "You make this old man wish he were thirty years younger. Richard, my lucky boy, you have found yourself a wonderful—''

"Why would you think you killed my uncle?" Prince Richard asked.

"You told me he was going to have a heart attack. I assumed it was because of the ring." Her heartbeat accelerated. The ring. She'd forgotten for a moment. Christina faced the prince, wishing he'd shown the same compassion and sincerity as his uncle, but all she saw was a scowl of impatience. How could she have ever mistaken him for Prince Charming? The two had nothing in common except the word "prince." The realization made her long for a familiar face. "Do you know where my father is?"

The marquess gave her shoulder a reassuring squeeze. "He should be along shortly."

"Take off the gloves," Prince Richard ordered.

"Really, my dear nephew," the marquess said. "Christina is not one of your subjects. She's going to be your—''

"Uncle Phillippe, please. If you feel the need to interfere, I will have to ask you to leave."

"I pretend to have a heart attack so you can clear the palace and this is what I get," the marquess said, sounding affronted.

"You pretended to have a heart attack?" Christina asked.

"Yes, my dear." The marquess winked. "And a valiant performance, worthy of an Oscar if I might say so myself."

"Why?"

Prince Richard cleared his throat.

The marquess sighed. "Why don't you ask His Serene Highness?"

Prince Richard said nothing. Who the hell did he think he was, standing there with an arrogant expression on his face as if she was a low-life serf? She'd cried thinking she'd been the cause of the marquess's heart attack. *Cried.*

She deserved an answer. Christina planted her hands on her hips. "So, are you going to tell me, Your Serene Highness?"

Both the marquess and Didier chuckled, earning them a glare from Prince Richard. He glanced toward the ceiling and let loose a tirade in French.

Pompous ass. As if I wanted to be part of this. She could match his colorful French vocabulary word for word, but she chose to take a calming breath instead. "Your Highness, I did not glue the ring to my finger, nor did I do any of this on purpose. If you have anything to say, please say it to my face in English."

Prince Richard studied her. "You speak French?"

"Fluently," she said, enjoying the surprise that registered in his eyes. The man had way too much pride. "When I was in college, I studied in Paris."

"Any other languages?"

"Italian." Christina realized she had the upper hand. And she liked it, liked it a lot. "I also spent two semesters in Florence."

"Your Highness," Didier said, rather bravely, Christina thought, "I believe Miss Armstrong is waiting for her answer about the marquess's heart attack."

"It looks as if you have two champions, Miss Armstrong." Prince Richard regained his princely composure, but a vein in his neck still throbbed. Not so cool and collected as he wanted people to believe. "You want to know, I shall tell you. Since you so inexcu—"

Didier coughed. "Excuse me, Your Highness."

Good thing looks couldn't kill or one of her champions would be a goner. Christina could have sworn she saw the prince sending daggers, machetes and a wood block full of Wusthof knives toward Didier.

Prince Richard continued. "Since you had the misfortune of getting the ring *stuck* on your finger, I felt it was in our mutual best interest to clear the palace before any gossip could occur. I needed a way to end the party, so I enlisted the aid of my thespian uncle.''

"I've done Shakespeare," the marquess said, giving a bow.

A man after her own heart. Christina chuckled.

"Thanks to his brilliant performance, I can see to...his recovery.''

See to *her* was what Prince Richard meant. His ruse. It had worked. Not a bad plan, she had to admit. And she was in favor of doing anything to stop gossip and keep the press at bay. His Serene Highness might not be a knight in shining armor, but he was quick on his feet. Maybe he could figure a way out of this mess.

"Now that I have answered your question, Miss Armstrong, would you kindly remove the gloves?''

A knock at the door stopped her. Silence. No one moved. Everyone stared at the door. Another knock.

Prince Richard nodded at Didier, who moved to the doors and opened one of them slightly before stepping back. "It's Mr. Armstrong.''

Her father entered the room with a smile on his face. Oh, no. Christina estimated that in less than sixty seconds his smile would turn upside down. She hid her hands behind her back.

"Sweetheart." Her father's hug took her by surprise. He not only preferred showing his affection with gifts rather than touch, but she expected him to be angry at her, not happy. "Sorry for the delay, Your Highness, but I had to telephone my wife.''

Mother knew. Christina wrung her hands. "How did she take...I mean... Is she okay?''

"She's fine.''

Fine? Her mother? *That* wasn't possible. The only reason her mother hadn't come to San Montico was because of the discovery of a new wrinkle that warranted an emergency appointment, complete with chartered jet and flight crew, to her plastic surgeon in Beverly Hills. Overreaction was Claire Armstrong's middle name.

"May I see the ring, Your Highness?" Alan asked.

Prince Richard nodded. "If Miss Armstrong removes the glove."

"Do as the prince says," her father whispered. "Whatever he says."

"Yes, sir." She removed the glove and held out her left hand.

"Interesting." Alan tugged and twisted it. She waited for him to yell at her, to express his disappointment with her yet again. Instead, his smile widened. "It's not coming off, is it?"

"No, it's not, Mr. Armstrong," Didier said. The marquess echoed him.

"It will come off." Prince Richard grimaced. "The ring does not fit."

The three other men exchanged a glance making Christina feel like the only one not privy to a secret handshake.

"I would like Christina to remain at the palace," Prince Richard said.

Say no, Daddy. Say no.

"That's understandable considering the circumstances," Alan replied. "I'll have her luggage packed and sent over. Discreetly, of course."

Prince Richard nodded his approval. "You are more than welcome to stay yourself."

Please stay, Daddy. Please stay.

"Thank you, Your Highness, but that isn't necessary." Alan glanced at the ring on her finger and chuckled. "I have so much to take care of I doubt I'll sleep a wink tonight."

Finally, he was going to do something. The overwhelming sense of relief made Christina sigh.

"Don't worry." Her father patted her arm. "I'll take care of everything."

Thank goodness. She wasn't in this alone. But her father was acting so calmly, so unlike his normal disapproving self. "You aren't mad?"

"A bit surprised," he admitted. "But not mad."

Now she really felt like the only one excluded from the club. Something was definitely going on.

"My uncle will see you out," Prince Richard said.

Christina wanted her father to stay. She wanted to tell him how much she appreciated his help. She wanted to tell him how much she loved him. She said good-night instead.

"Sleep well." Alan kissed the top of her head. "I'm so proud of you, sweetheart."

Christina stared, dumbfounded. She'd waited for years to hear her father say those words. All she ever wanted was to be a good girl and make her parents proud, but things had never worked out that way. She got into trouble without even trying. Getting the ring stuck on her finger was a perfect example. Except for keeping it a secret from the press, how was this any different from the times before?

Richard would not give up. So much was at stake, but nothing had worked. Not the soap, not the lotion, not the Vaseline. The ring was still stuck. He was running out of ideas.

And time.

It was almost two o'clock in the morning. He had kept his mother and the entire palace in the dark about Christina and the ring. He could not keep it hidden forever. Come morning, the dawn would bring the truth about the ring and who wore it to light.

If the citizens thought the "magic" of the ring had selected Christina to be his bride and Richard married her, they would cling to their silly customs and traditions even more. The legend would not only seal his fate, but that of San Montico. With archaic ideas such as legends and fairy tales part of everyday life, San Montico would never have true modernization. His father's wish would go unfulfilled. Richard could not let that happen.

He reached into the back of a cabinet and pulled out a bottle of oil. "We shall try this, Miss Armstrong."

Lifting her hand from the sink full of ice, Christina leaned against the bathroom counter. "Go ahead, Your Highness, but since it looks like this ring isn't coming off in the near future, you might as well start calling me Christina. And you, too, Didier."

Standing next to Richard, Didier smiled. "Christina is such a lovely name. A name fit for a princess."

Princess Christina? Richard grimaced. Didier was up to his old tricks. His matchmaking would not work. Christina would not become Richard's wife; she would not become Her Serene Highness of San Montico. The ring on her finger meant nothing, as did the legend. Only he could decide who became the next princess. It was not going to be Christina Armstrong.

And having Didier around displaying his not-so-subtle approval of her only complicated matters further. Richard scowled. "Leave us, Didi."

"But the ring, Your Highness?"

"I will see to it." Richard opened the bottle of oil. "You need to sleep. Tomorrow will be a busy day."

Didier nodded. "I will have a room prepared for Christina, Your Highness."

"She is staying here."

"Here?" Christina stiffened. "I can't sleep here."

"I cannot sleep here, *Your Highness,*" Richard corrected her lapse. "May I ask why?"

Her eyes widened at his question. "Because, *Your Highness,* this is your room. Where would you sleep?"

"Why here, of course." Richard laughed at the indignant look on her face, the surprised tone of her voice. She did have a sort of innocent charm. An act, he was certain. Americans would do anything to gain a royal title. His ex-fiancée had taught him a painful yet valuable lesson. "Christina, the ring has been in my family for generations, centuries, actually. I prefer to remain near it."

"You can lock me in a room, in the tower even, place a guard outside my door. I'm not going anywhere, Your Highness. I promise."

Her promises meant nothing to him. Besides, he could not risk having his mother see a guard standing watch over one of the guest rooms. She would know something was wrong. And if she found out about the ring... The wedding invitations would be in the mail by tomorrow afternoon. "You are staying here. With me."

She started to speak, then stopped.

Didier frowned. "Your Highness—"

"Good night, Didi."

"Didier," Christina said, "thanks for your help."

"The pleasure was mine. Happy birthday, Your Highness." Didier bowed, then left the bathroom.

Some birthday. A trip to the salt mines of Siberia would be better than this. Anything would be.

But Richard was here with Christina, who wore the royal engagement ring. If the news got out, he would be married to her by this time next week.

Married to a stranger. An American, no less. Under the guise of the legend and true love. No way. He had to get the ring off her finger. Now. Richard grabbed Christina's hand.

"Ow."

He released her hand. He shouldn't have been so rough. "I'm...I only wanted to try the oil."

She studied him, her arched brows drawn together. Two small lines formed above the bridge of her nose. "Look, I want to get this ring off as badly as *you* do." With a slight hesitation, she offered her hand. "Oil me up, Your Highness."

Disrespectful, but kind of cute. Perhaps another time, another place. Absurd. Unknowingly or not, she had been drawn into the legend. After he removed the ring, Richard never wanted to see Christina Armstrong again.

Tilting the bottle, he poured oil on her finger, set the bottle on the counter and reached for the ring. His large hand engulfed her small, delicate one. As he rubbed the oil around the gold band, she jerked away.

Her cheeks rosy, she stared at him. "I can do it myself, Your Highness."

"No. I will."

Defiance flickered in her eyes, but she held out her hand anyway. At least she knew how to obey. Slowly, he rubbed on the oil, making sure he didn't miss a spot. He had not noticed before, but her fingernails were painted a pale pink with white tips. Just like his mother used to wear before his father died.

But a French manicure did not make a princess.

"What is this?" Christina asked.

Once again, she forgot to address him as "Your Highness." "Oil."

With her right hand, she picked up the bottle. Her eyes widened. "It's...massage oil?"

She needed a lesson in royal protocol. "Yes."

"Figures." She set the bottle on the counter. "Do you usually keep a large supply of massage oil on hand, Your Highness? Or did we just luck out tonight?"

She was the most aggravating woman he had ever met. He continued rubbing. "It was a gift."

"I'm sure it was."

Ignoring her suggestive tone, Richard reminded himself she was an American and did not know better. He tried moving the ring, but it still would not budge. Unwilling to give up, he added more oil. His fingers glided over hers, the friction of their skin warmed the oil oozing between their hands.

Soft. Even the coldness of her iced hand could not hide how satiny her skin felt beneath his fingertips. The smell of vanilla drifted up. No wonder Didier had wanted to stay and help. This was quite enjoyable. Richard stared at her reflection in the mirror until she blinked and looked away.

So did he.

He should not be enjoying this. This was not a game or foreplay. Christina's skin was not soft. Any woman's hand would feel soft with a bottle of massage oil rubbed on it.

He tried the ring again.

Nothing.

He needed to think of something—a new tactic. Maybe he needed to work on her swollen knuckle. Yes, he would try that.

Letting the oil act as a lubricant, Richard massaged her knuckle. This would certainly do the trick. Christina did have long, elegant fingers. Moving to another knuckle, he wondered if she ever painted her nails red.

His gaze locked with hers.

"Uh, Your Highness," she said, her cheeks flushed, "that's the wrong finger."

Richard let go of her hand as if it were a stick of dynamite ready to blow. He couldn't explain his lapse nor why he felt as if he were ten years old and his mother had caught him playing with his great-great-grandfather's jewel-encrusted sword.

"I'll try it." Christina pulled on the ring. "It's still stuck, Your Highness."

And so was he.

As long as the ring was on Christina's finger, he was stuck with her.

She washed her hands. "My finger's really swollen. I don't think it's coming off tonight, Your Highness."

They had been at it so long. Too long. Richard noticed the dark circles under Christina's eyes. "We will wait until morning to try again. You must be tired."

The edges of her mouth turned up slightly. "I am, Your Highness, but if you wish to continue, I understand. I know you want your ring back."

The genuine tone of her voice surprised him, as did her willingness to continue even though she was exhausted. He was used to people wanting things from him. Few ever offered to give anything in return.

"No, we shall wait." He noticed her gown, now wrinkled and showing signs of the long evening. She could not sleep in it. "I will find you something to wear."

She wiped her hands on a towel. "My dress is fine, Your Highness."

The tight-fitting bodice pushed her breasts up and tapered to a V that accentuated her hourglass curves. "Actually, it is lovely, but I am sure the designer did not intend it to be worn to bed. Come with me." Richard opened the mahogany armoire in his bedroom. He searched through the clothes and pulled a button-down hunter-green pajama top from the hanger. "Wear this."

She ran her fingertips over the fabric. "It's silk, Your Highness."

"Yes. Is there a problem?"

"No, it's beautiful," she said. "I just don't want to ruin it. Couldn't I borrow a T-shirt?"

"You will not ruin it."

"That's what they all say," she mumbled before walking into the bathroom and closing the door.

Realizing he could not sleep as he normally did, he quickly changed into the matching pajama bottoms. Richard had not worn pajamas in years, just as he had never allowed a woman to spend the entire night with him in this suite. Well, he had never turned thirty before or had his engagement ring stuck on an American's finger, either.

A night of firsts.

He wished it were over.

The bathroom door opened. Christina stepped out, carrying her gown and matching pumps. The only thing he could see were her bare feet with her toenails painted a shocking pink. She laid the gown on a nearby chair, bent down and set her shoes on the floor.

As she stood by his bed, Richard sucked in a breath, unable to stop himself from staring at her. Christina's auburn hair fell past her shoulders, gently framing her face. Her beautiful face. The silky fabric brushed against the curves underneath. Her womanly curves. The pajama top fell midthigh on a pair of perfectly shaped legs. Her long legs. "You...you can have it now, Your Highness."

He wanted it all right. He wanted...

Her.

He could not explain the rush of desire, the overwhelming sense of needing her, but he did not care. She was here; he was here. Why not make the best of a bad situation? After all, it was his birthday. He smiled at Christina.

Princess material, no. Lover material, yes.

Chapter Three

Prince Richard hadn't said a word, but Christina could see it, feel it. While she'd been in the bathroom, he'd become the dashing prince she'd met in the grand hallway, the sexy prince who had set her heart aflutter.

His smile made her feel like the only piece of chocolate decadence at a Weight Watchers meeting. Chocolate that was starting to melt under his intense stare full of longing, desire, need. His gaze lingered, practically caressed, making her feel like a desirable woman.

And she resented it. Resented how she felt her own resolve weakening.

But she couldn't help herself.

This man could steal any woman's heart if he set his mind to it.

But not *her* heart, she reminded herself.

To be honest, she preferred his majestic scowl to the come-hither curve gracing his lips.

Lips made for nibbling, tasting, kissing.

Wait. They were only lips. Princely lips she didn't want

to have anything to do with. So what if his less-than-appealing personality didn't diminish his sex appeal?

She wasn't interested. Period.

And if she told herself that enough, she might eventually believe it. Not that it mattered, of course. She was simply overreacting, letting her imagination and hormones run wild.

The prince hadn't propositioned her; he hadn't said one word. Teasing—that's what he was doing—teasing her to get a reaction. Those bedroom eyes meant nothing. Nothing at all.

Besides, Prince Richard didn't like her; he was angry at her. She wore his ring. Maybe not actually wore, but the ring was on her finger. Didn't he remember?

His smile widened, deepening the faint lines at the corners of his eyes. Apparently, he'd forgotten about the ring. Temporary insanity. Or...

No, it couldn't be.

But he was staring and smiling at her. A seductive smile designed to make any woman swoon. Maybe he did want to touch her, kiss her, make love to her.

Maybe she was blowing this out of proportion. Or maybe she had something on her face. She touched her cheek. "Is anything wrong, Your Highness?"

"No." He took a step closer.

Christina gulped, feeling way out of her league. Especially with him wearing those pajama bottoms. His green silk pants left just enough to her imagination to make her want to see if what was under the fabric was as perfect as his defined abs, his wide shoulders and his not-overmuscled, but not-an-ounce-of-flab chest.

Typical vain man. Prancing around his bedroom like a Chippendale dancer. Okay standing, not prancing. "Can't you put your top on?"

"You are wearing it," he said.

The intimacy of wearing a matched set, something she imagined happening when she married someday, made her swallow hard. "I..."

"Are you offering me yours?"

"No." She paused long enough to see his smile widen further. Uh-oh. His adorable dimple was back. "Don't you have another pair?"

"Normally, I do not sleep in pajamas."

Just what she needed to hear to send her imagination into overdrive. And into overdrive it went. What would it feel like to run her hands over the golden hair covering his Michelangelo-sculpted chest? To have his strong arms pick her up and carry her to the giant bed, a bed made for lovers?

Stop. Right now.

She shouldn't be thinking like that. Not here, locked in a room—make that *bed*room—with a half-naked, gorgeous prince. Christina wrapped her arms around her waist and inched away from the bed.

His bed.

Show him the ring. That will erase the smile from his face, the desire—make that lust—in his eyes.

But she couldn't do anything except stare back entranced, hypnotized by the prince's piercing gaze, by his incredible physique. She wanted to touch him, to see if he was real.

He took another step toward her. "Silk suits you, Christina."

A compliment? Her pulse raced, speeding faster than the winning car at Indy. She stepped back and bumped into the wall. Trapped. Nowhere to go. She should be more worried than she was. "Thank you, Your Highness."

Her words sounded husky. Nothing like her normal voice. What was wrong with her? Nerves? She wet her Sahara-dry lips.

"When we are alone, you may call me Richard."

Richard? She wouldn't; she couldn't.

He closed the distance between them. Her pulse broke the land-speed record. She glanced at the bed, then back at him. "Where, er, where should I...?"

Words failed her. The nearness of him left her tongue-tied.

"Where should you sleep?" He finished the question for her.

She nodded, not trusting her own voice. Not trusting herself.

His eyes twinkled with anticipation. "Where would you like to sleep?"

Talk about a loaded question. Her answer could get her into more trouble. Christina merely shrugged, fighting the urge to tremble as he moved even closer.

"The bed is big enough for two."

No, it wasn't. All she needed to make her trip to San Montico a complete disaster was to wake up and find herself tangled in the sheets, legs entwined, her head against his bare chest. Her father had told her to obey Prince Richard, but she didn't think this was what he had in mind. Christina pressed her sweaty palms against the wall. "I'm used to sleeping alone."

He raised an eyebrow.

"Not really alone," she admitted. "I mean, I sleep with Francis."

"Frances?"

"My cat, and it's Francis with an *i*."

"You have a male cat."

"No." Christina couldn't think straight, not with Prince Richard so close. Don't think about him. Think about Francis. "She's female, but I promised my grandfather I would name my first pet after Frank Sinatra. I myself felt compelled to name her after a character in Shakespeare, which gave me quite a dilemma.''

"So you came up with Francis.''

"Yes, but it wasn't easy.'' Neither was this. Richard's spicy scent filled her nostrils. So earthy, so sensual, so male. Forget about him. "It was dumb luck I found a minor character named Francis in *King Henry IV, Part 1*. Did you know he's the only character in the entire Shakespearean canon named Francis?''

"I did not.'' Prince Richard reached for her collar, straightening it. His warm fingers brushed her skin, sending a shiver of sensation down her spine. "Francis is a lucky kitty.''

So am I. Christina bit the inside of her cheek.

Prince Richard ran his fingertips down the lapel, stopping when he reached the first button. "Tell me more about Francis.''

Christina didn't want to think about what he was doing, about what she wanted him to do. "She's cute—a tabby with calico spots and white fur on her chin and belly.'' Christina watched with anticipation as he ran his fingertips along the circumference of the silk-covered button. "She's a good cat. When I rub her belly, she purrs like an engine.''

Prince Richard flashed her a devastating grin that made her want to meow. "Belly rubs work wonders.''

"Yes, they…''

Warning bells sounded inside her head. *You almost meowed, for heaven's sake. Get away from him. Now.*

Christina searched for a way out, an escape route. She saw nothing except two leather chairs in front of the fireplace. They would have to do. "About our sleeping arrangements, *Your Highness*. I can sleep on one of the chairs or on the floor.''

"The floor?'' Prince Richard laughed. "That would be so uncomfortable. Surely we can do better than that.''

Not if she had any say in the matter. Christina stepped around him and moved toward the chairs. "That's okay, Your, er, Highness. You wouldn't believe some of the places I've bedded down, I mean, slept." Needing to shut up before she said something stupid, she faked a yawn. "I'm really tired."

"If you are tired, it should not matter if we share the bed."

"It would matter," she said a little too quickly. "I mean—"

"What do you mean, Christina?"

Her name rolled from his lips with the slight hint of a French accent. She loved the way he said her name. No, she hated it. "I toss and turn. And I snore."

"Did Francis tell you that?"

Damn. Caught in her own trap. She never could tell even the smallest of white lies. Her cheeks warmed. Only a soft knock on the door saved her from further embarrassment.

"Who is it?" Prince Richard asked, sounding impatient.

"Your mother," a female voice answered.

His mother? That could only mean one thing—trouble. Christina exchanged a panicked look with Prince Richard.

"Just a minute," he said to his mother, then turned to Christina. "Hide."

"Where?"

He glanced at the bathroom and another door. "If my mother finds you here..."

The beautiful Princess Marguerite probably wouldn't understand why Christina was in the prince's room at this late hour and wearing his pajama top.

He opened the doors to his armoire and pointed. Looking inside the wardrobe, Christina hesitated. "In there?"

"Richard?" Princess Marguerite called out. "I must speak with you immediately."

He tensed. Without a second thought, Christina climbed

in, moving aside the tails of shirts hanging side by side. Prince Richard rolled her gown and tossed it to her. He closed the armoire, leaving her in darkness.

The cramped armoire smelled like cedar. She clutched her gown to her chest. A tight fit, but it worked. For the time being. "Don't forget my shoes, Your Highness."

"Richard? Open this door," his mother said.

He messed his hair, rumpled the sheets and kicked Christina's pumps under the bed before unlocking the door. "Good evening, Mother."

Marguerite pushed her way into the room. Her black gown swished against the Savonnerie carpet. "I hope I did not interrupt anything."

"No, I was in bed."

"Alone?" She peered around him to stare at his bed.

Her question did not deserve an answer. She always seemed disappointed when she failed to find a woman spending the night. It meant waiting that much longer for grandchildren. "I thought you would be asleep by now, Mother."

"How could I sleep after what happened tonight? I want to know what's going on, Richard." Crossing the room, she glanced in the bathroom. "And do not tell me you evacuated the palace because of your uncle's heart attack. I know he was pretending."

"He was not pretending." Richard saw the contrast of green against the black of the bed skirt. One of Christina's pumps stuck out from under his bed. Damn. "He simply mistook a bout of indigestion for the real thing."

"He ruined your party."

While his mother peered inside his walk-in closet, Richard nudged the shoe farther under his bed. "He thought he was having a heart attack, Mother. Surely his health is more important than a party?"

"But the ring." She shut the closet door. "There were

so many lovely young women present at the ball. I was hoping you would find *her* tonight."

"I am sorry to disappoint you."

"It's not your fault the ring didn't fit any of the women or the party was cut short."

"Fate seems to have conspired against me."

It most definitely had. A piece of green fabric—Christina's gown?—stuck out of the bottom of his armoire. His mother had not seen it. Yet.

"I simply wanted you to experience the same love and happiness the Legend of the Ring brought your father and me."

"Happiness, Mother?" Richard could not believe he was hearing this. He hurried to the armoire. Leaning against it, he struck a casual pose and hid the fabric with his heel. "For the past ten years, you have done nothing but wear black and mourn him."

"I miss him, Richard, but do not forget we had twenty-one years of joy before his death. I will always have the memories, and I have the ring to thank for that."

A ring could not bring happiness, true love, no matter how much his mother wanted to believe it. Just listening to her... She spoke as if she had died, too. She sounded so sad. The way she had sounded since his father's death. Richard blamed her sorrow on the Legend of the Ring. "Why not experience that joy again, Mother? You can fall in love and remarry."

As his mother moved closer to him and the armoire, her smile disappeared. "The love your father and I shared...I cannot replace that with another. I would not even want to try. But I do want you to marry and provide me with the grandchildren I so long to have."

He knew how much his mother wanted him to marry, to produce an heir—grandchildren. Talking about the legend and his birthday ball had brought the light back to her eyes. Now it was gone.

Completely.

What kind of son was he, putting his wants ahead of his mother's? He did not want to know the answer.

"Where is the ring?"

Torn between his own happiness and hers, Richard hesitated. All he had to do was show her the ring on Christina's finger. His mother would be thrilled, and he would be...

He could not. If he caved in and married because of the legend, he would live to regret it. He had to break the de Thierry tie to the Legend of the Ring. Not only for himself, but for future generations.

The pursuit of a wife had taught him "one true love" and "happily ever after" existed only in fairy tales and fantasies. Not even an enchanted ring could change that.

"Do you have the ring, Richard?"

"No, Didier has it." The lie came so easily.

"Well, at the very least, I can wear it again."

"No."

Her blue eyes widened. "You do not want me to wear it?"

Richard had been too harsh. He hated disappointing his mother; the last thing he wanted to do was hurt her. She was the one woman who loved him for who he was— simply her son. His title did not matter, nor did his faults. "So many women tried on the ring tonight, I want to have it cleaned first."

The tenderness in her eyes made Richard swallow the guilt lodged in his throat. She caressed his cheek. "You are always one step ahead of me, my son. Just like your father."

The comparison to his father made Richard feel like a cad. His father had been a respectable and honorable man. Richard was neither. A battle of duties raged inside him.

Duty to his country or duty to himself. Had his father ever felt so torn? "I try my best."

"You do better than try." She kissed his cheek. "Happy birthday, Richard."

"Thank you, Mother. For the ball and...everything."

"It has been a long evening." She stifled a yawn. "I will see you in the morning."

"Good night." Richard escorted her out of his room, closed the door and locked it. He hated lying to his mother, but he had no choice. He had to keep the ring on Christina's finger a secret. It wasn't as if the ring fit her. It did not; it was only stuck. But all San Montico wanted him to marry. He could not let them think the legend had come true.

He had always done what was expected of him. Until now. Surely his mother would understand. And he would make it up to her. He would.

Opening the armoire doors, Richard expected Christina to rush out. But she did not. She did not move at all. Curled up with her gown on her lap and her eyes closed, Christina slept soundly, oblivious to everything. He stared at her.

Lovely.

But off-limits.

He would not act on his physical urges, on his lust. Richard was above that; he was a de Thierry prince. No need to let raging testosterone rule him. His sudden attraction to her made no sense, given the circumstances. Besides, he could have any woman he wanted, whenever he wanted.

But he needed to find the right one.

If only there had not been so much pressure to find the perfect wife for himself and the perfect princess for San Montico. If only his pursuit had not been so heartbreakingly fruitless. If only there wasn't the legend...

Lifting Christina from the armoire, Richard caught a whiff of grapefruit—her shampoo, perhaps?

She stirred and blinked her eyes open. "What—"

"Go back to sleep," he said.

Christina closed her eyes.

He carried her to the bed and gently set her down. Her copper hair spread over the pillow like strands of silk; her chest rose and fell with even breaths. A serene smile graced her lips. As he covered her with his comforter, Richard's gaze focused on the royal engagement ring. His engagement ring. He wanted it back. Now.

Her finger looked less swollen. Maybe the ring would slide off. Just maybe. Impatient, Richard lifted her hand. He tried the ring.

Damn.

He tugged harder.

Nothing.

Christina pulled her hand away. He waited for her to open her eyes, but she did not. Instead, an intriguing smile formed on her lips, lips begging to be kissed.

Richard froze; his groin tightened. Was she having a pleasant dream or was she pretending to be asleep? He should not care either way. Tempted or not, removing the ring from her finger was his only priority. Nothing else. Not even those full pink lips.

Christina snuggled against the down pillow, creating an inviting picture of what a night spent in bed with her might be like. Something about her…

This was the woman San Montico would want him to marry in a week. Thinking in those terms made it easy to walk away from the bed and flick off the lights. He sat in one of the leather antique reading chairs and closed his eyes. Some birthday this turned out to be.

Sunlight warmed Christina's cheeks, but she didn't want to open her eyes. She longed to return to her magical dream of the knight in shining armor who had taken her hand in his and pledged his undying love.

Too bad it was only a dream.

Christina opened her eyes, adjusting to the light streaming through the windows. Another sunny day. The chirping song of a bird drifted inside. She stretched her arms over her head. A quick shower and she could pack for her flight home.

And then Christina realized where she was. Not the luxurious hotel suite she shared with her father. But the palace. Prince Richard's bedroom. Prince Richard's bed.

How did she get here? The last thing she remembered was hiding in the armoire. She must have fallen asleep, and Prince Richard must have carried her to bed.

Christina bolted upright. No sign of the prince. Only... She covered her mouth with her hand. It wasn't a faceless knight in her dream, but the prince. Fantasy and reality had merged leaving her more confused about Prince Richard than ever. Being attracted to him was one thing—his not-so-charming personality made up for that—but dreaming about him? It wouldn't do, not at all.

She heard quiet voices coming from the bathroom. Did he have a servant draw his bath and help him dress? And what if Prince Richard wasn't dressed? All she needed was to have him saunter out wearing only a towel or worse, nothing.

The bathroom door opened. An attractive, dark-skinned woman with razor-clipped black hair walked out followed by two twenty-something-looking women with to-die-for hair. "Good morning, Ms. Armstrong, I am Delia. These are my assistants, Elise and Faye."

Feeling underdressed with these fashion plates standing next to the bed, she pulled the comforter to her waist. "Uh, hello."

Delia held a clear clipboard in her hand, but with her red miniskirt and blouse she didn't look like a housekeeper or maid. At least not the kind Christina's mother employed. "Did you sleep well?"

She didn't know why Delia wanted to know. And who were Elise and Faye? Runway models or soap-opera actresses? "I slept fine, thanks."

"Are you ready?" Delia asked, a hint of expectation in her voice.

Oh, no. Realization hit Christina like the blade of the guillotine against Marie Antoinette's neck. These women were going to prepare her to have her finger chopped off. It was the only thing that made sense. Her finger was a goner.

Christina retrieved the gloves from the nightstand with her right hand. She drew them under the covers and slipped the gloves onto her hands.

Play dumb. Pretend you don't know what's going on. "Ready for what?"

"To have your measurements taken." Delia's wide smile showed two perfect rows of pearly white teeth. With her high cheekbones and exotic features, she could have stepped out of the pages of *Vogue*. "We must start work on your gown if we are to finish on time."

Measurements? A gown? What about her finger? Maybe Christina was still dreaming. "I don't understand."

Faye, wearing a mustard-yellow pantsuit that would have overwhelmed or washed out any other woman, stepped forward. "Didn't His Highness tell you we were coming?"

"No, he didn't."

Brows furrowed, the three women glanced at each other. Elise murmured something. Delia brushed aside the concern with a wave of her hand, leaving a light scent of sandalwood and vanilla in the air. "No matter. I can understand his lapse now that I've seen you myself. His Highness would have had other things on his mind. He is a man after all." Her mouth formed an O; she lowered her gaze. "Ms.

Armstrong, forgive me. I shouldn't have spoken that way about Prince Richard."

"Don't worry about it," Christina reassured Delia, liking her more and more as each minute passed. "My friends and I joke about men all the time. We call the Y chromosome a genetic mutation. A mistake or a bad joke depending on your perspective."

Looking relieved, Delia smiled. "The marquess was correct."

"Excuse me?"

"He said you would be good for San Montico. I see what he meant." Delia snapped her fingers. "Let's get started."

Elise pulled a cloth tape measure from her pocket. Faye held out swatches of fabric. The three women stared at her.

Guess it's time to get up. Christina crawled out of bed. Faye held fabric swatches against Christina's face and hair.

As Elise called out the bust and waist measurements, Delia wrote them down. "We will have to design a gown to accentuate your curves."

Christina blushed. "I appreciate the offer of a gown, but I cannot accept one."

Elise and Faye gasped. Delia frowned. "But I thought..."

Christina pointed to her crumpled dress on the chair. Prince Richard must have laid it out. "I have the gown I wore last night."

"It's beautiful, but you can't wear it again," Delia said. "And green would never do."

"It won't?" Christina asked. She liked green.

"No. It would cause a scandal." Faye showed her a swatch of white silk. "What do you think of this?"

Christina ran her fingertips over the exquisite fabric. "It's lovely, but I cannot—"

"I think you'd look beautiful in the natural silk," Faye said.

"But the color?" Christina asked.

Delia made pencil marks on the clipboard. "Ivory is an acceptable choice, but most brides prefer wearing white."

Bride?

"Of course," Delia said, "it's your wedding gown and we want to make you happy."

Christina couldn't have heard her correctly. "My w-w-wedding gown?"

"Hard to believe, isn't it? The whole island is so excited. We've been waiting a long time for this." Delia smiled and hugged the clipboard to her chest. "Just think, in a week you'll be married to Prince Richard."

Elise sighed. "We'll be calling you Princess Christina."

Princess Christina? Married to Prince Richard? In a week?

Her knees buckled. Christina reached for the bed for support. Her gaze locked on the glove about to fall off her left hand.

The ring. It had to be the stupid ring.

She hit the floor with a thud. Ignoring the concerns of the other women, Christina pulled the glove up. She rose, straightened her pajama top and rubbed her aching hip. What was another bruise when her life was about to be ruined?

A wedding? Impossible.

She couldn't marry Prince Richard; she'd just met him. To be honest, he might be drop-dead gorgeous, but she didn't like his arrogant personality and the way he ordered everyone around. Besides, he'd never proposed. Not that she would ever say yes. Marriage to him was out of the question. She wanted to marry a man with a normal, everyday job. A man who wasn't hounded by the press over everything he did or said. A man who had calluses on his hands and knew what it was to work hard.

Definitely not a prince.

There had to be a mistake. Time to find Prince Richard and put a stop to this. If her father found out...

Chapter Four

Standing in the salon, Richard stared at the frenzy outside the palace gate. Paparazzi. At least fifty people—cameras, video recorders and microphones in hand—clamored for a front row spot. A helicopter circled noisily overhead.

So much for keeping the ring and Christina a secret.

Tension knotted his gut. Not even the sweet fragrance of his mother's rose garden drifting in through the open window eased his frustration. Damn Uncle Phillippe for telling not only the world but Richard's mother. If ever the palace needed a tower or a dungeon, it was now.

"Following the nuptial mass, we can have a parade through the village in a horse-drawn carriage, then a dinner and ball at the palace." His mother's joy rang out in her voice. "Oh, and a fireworks display. That would be the perfect way to end the day."

"Don't forget ice sculptures," Uncle Phillippe added. "I do love ice sculptures. They are so…icy."

"Fireworks would be spectacular and ice sculptures are a must," Alan Armstrong agreed.

"We should have thirty ice sculptures," Didier said. "One for each illustrious year of Prince Richard's life."

Unbelievable. Didier was participating in the madness. Stepping away from the window, Richard glanced at the people planning his wedding—or rather his "nuptials" as his mother preferred to call it. Each glowed with an excitement more contagious than a winter flu. Even Alan Armstrong, the billionaire businessman, was getting carried away with the royal wedding plans. Not even he could remain detached from the flurry of insanity.

Chaos outside, chaos inside. Richard was the only sane person left on the island. The urge to sail away on his yacht was becoming stronger and stronger, but he couldn't leave. He had a duty, a responsibility to stay and see this through.

Uncle Phillippe clapped his hands together. "Doves. We must release a flock of doves."

Everyone else nodded their agreement, and Didier wrote a note to check the availability of doves.

Richard rolled his eyes. Although the four sat on settees and chairs, they might as well be wearing black robes and white wigs, presiding at the high court and condemning him to a life sentence of marriage.

If this were a war, he would be losing. All his troops would have retreated, leaving him to fight on his own. But he was far from surrendering.

He had to find a way out.

Richard began pacing. His heels rang out against the hardwood floor.

Marguerite sighed. "Oh, Richard, sit down."

Sit? At a time like this? Life as he knew it was over. He stopped pacing and stared at her.

"Do not give me that look, my son." She pursed her lips. "I should be the one upset. I cannot believe you did not tell me, but I suppose a mother is always the last to know."

How could people not understand what was happening? He clenched his hand into a fist. "The ring is merely stuck on Christina's finger. It does not fit."

"Of course not, Your Highness." Uncle Phillippe grinned.

Alan chuckled. "If you say so, Your Highness."

His mother laughed. "Isn't he just adorable?"

"The ring will come off," Richard said.

Didier smiled, an infuriating smile that made Richard want to forget his advisor was also his oldest and dearest friend. "The legend says the ring will come off once the couple realize their true love for one another, Your Highness."

True love did not exist. He and Christina would never be a couple. "The legend is nothing more than a fairy tale made up by overly romantic, matchmaking mothers."

"We mothers need something to do with our time."

"I can find my own bride."

Marguerite tsked. "You had thirty years to find a woman of your choosing, Richard. The choice is no longer yours to make. The ring has found you a bride. All that's left is for you to fall in love."

Never.

"Once you spend a little time with Christina, Your Highness, I'm sure you'll feel differently." Alan smiled. "She's a sweet young woman. A tad accident-prone, but with the right precautions everything will be fine."

Marguerite rubbed her palms together. "I can't wait to meet her."

As Alan described his daughter, Richard pulled Didier aside. "You must help me. This has nothing to do with any legend."

"Whether you believe in the legend or not is a moot point, Your Highness," Didier said. "Christina is wearing the ring. Nothing else is required by law."

Standing at the altar with Christina at his side was be-coming more and more of a reality, Richard realized. Fact and fiction had merged for everyone else in the room. And that meant one thing. If his family was serious about the wedding, then the citizens of San Montico would be, too.

He had to do something.

He had made a promise to his father, and Richard would see it was fulfilled. That meant proving the legend wrong, but how?

He rubbed his chin, and his fingertips scraped the night's growth of stubble. He had forgotten to shave. He never forgot to shave. This whole episode was turning him inside out, but he had to remain in control.

A setback, yes. But one setback would not stop him.

A liveried footman opened the salon doors. Christina stepped inside, her cheeks flushed. She wore his silk pajama top and the baggy white gloves on her hands.

"Your Highness, I've been all over the palace looking for you. There's been a terrible misunderstanding. Three women came to your room to measure me for a wed... Daddy?"

Like a volcano about to erupt, Alan stood. His face reddened. "You've been wandering around dressed like that?"

Richard could only imagine how many of the staff had seen her or what they thought of the half-dressed, sleep-rumpled, barefoot American searching the palace for him. Too late to worry about it now. Maybe someday he would be able to laugh about it. Then again...

"The color is quite becoming," Marguerite commented. "Wouldn't you agree, Alan?"

The question gave Christina's father time to regain his composure. "Yes, Your Highness, I do."

Richard appreciated his mother's efforts to diffuse an awkward situation, but that still did not explain Christina's unexpected appearance or her lack of appropriate apparel.

Leave it to an American. "What was so urgent that you needed to see me without taking the time to dress?"

"I'm sorry, Your Highness, but I panicked." She tugged on her left glove. "I didn't think about what I was wearing. I had to find you and clear up the misunderstanding about the women measuring me for a w-w-wedding gown."

He felt his own face redden. "Mother."

"Now, Richard," Marguerite said as if commissioning the design of a wedding dress were an everyday occurrence. "We only have a week. Delia's going to be working around the clock in order to finish on time. I didn't want to waste a single minute."

"Delia is an up-and-coming fashion designer," Uncle Phillippe explained to Alan. "I cannot wait to see her design for Christina's wedding gown."

Christina stepped closer. "But I don't need a wedding gown."

"You're wearing the ring," Marguerite said.

Christina's eyes widened. "You know about the ring, Your Highness?"

Marguerite nodded. "And most of San Montico, too."

"Well, you see, the ring is stuck on my finger. That's all." Christina hid her hands behind her back. "It'll come off."

Perhaps with Christina's explanation, people would see the truth. Richard could only hope.

"What about the legend?" Uncle Phillippe asked.

Christina drew her brows together. "What legend?"

All eyes focused on her. Richard's, too. "The Legend of the Ring."

She shrugged.

How could she not know? Richard did not understand. "Everyone knows about the legend. It's been in all the newspapers and magazines."

"I stay clear of any—"

Alan cleared his throat. "The press has been less than kind to our entire family, especially Christina since she is my only child and heir and prefers the more common things in life. She distances herself from such...drivel."

Everyone in the room nodded their understanding. Everyone, but Richard. "So you know nothing of the legend?"

"Nothing, Your Highness," she stated.

"Perhaps you should explain the Legend of the Ring, Your Highness," Didier suggested.

"Yes, dear." Marguerite clasped her hands and placed them gracefully in her lap. "Tell her."

Richard scowled. "Since this is so near and dear to your heart, Didi, *you* tell Christina about the so-called legend."

"I would be honored, Your Highness." As usual, Didier was caught up in the pomp and circumstance of all that was outdated and meaningless. "Centuries ago, a de Thierry prince swore he never would marry because he could not find a woman he loved. Not even among the most beautiful maidens or European royalty. His worried mother had to ensure her son marry and produce an heir. She had an enchantress cast a magic spell over the engagement ring. The spell guaranteed the ring would only fit the prince's one true love.

"His mother gave him the ring with a challenge attached. If the ring did not fit any of the women on the island by midnight on the day of his thirtieth birthday, she promised never to bother him again about marrying and providing an heir. But if the ring did fit, the prince would have to marry the woman or abdicate the throne to his younger, rebellious brother.

"The prince, known for his arrogance, agreed to his mother's challenge. On the night of his thirtieth birthday, the daughter of a visiting merchant tried on the ring and could not remove it."

Christina's eyes sparkled. "So I'm not the only one to get an engagement ring stuck on my finger."

"No, you are not the only one," Marguerite said.

Christina sighed. "Thank goodness."

Didier continued. "The prince fought the marriage, but the idea of losing the throne to his poor excuse of a brother made him reconsider and marry the woman."

"How did she get the ring off her finger?" Christina asked.

"The prince fell in love with his new princess. As soon as he admitted his love, the ring came off."

"And they had six children," Marguerite added. "Six."

"It's a charming tale, but the legend isn't real." Christina searched everyone's face for the truth. "It's just a...legend."

"Precisely." Richard crossed his arms. At least Christina had the sense not to believe in legends and magic. "A bunch of hocus-pocus nonsense. That is all."

"Tell her the truth," Marguerite said.

He hesitated. "The legend is not true, but the people of San Montico believe it is true. Therein lies the problem."

"What problem?" Christina asked.

"This should be interesting," Marguerite murmured. Didier chuckled in reply. Uncle Phillippe grinned at Alan.

Richard could not say the words. He stared up at the lavishly gilded domed ceiling. "Didi."

"You must marry Prince Richard in a week or he loses his throne," Didier said. "He will be forced to abdicate in favor of his uncle, the marquess."

Christina gasped. "That's...that's silly."

Marguerite laughed. "Richard, she is simply adorable. A bit outspoken, but we can work on that."

"Work on what?" Christina took a deep breath and exhaled slowly. "I admit it's a romantic tale, Your Highness, but we're not living in the Middle Ages. People don't get married because of an old legend. I've never heard anything more ridiculous.''

Beauty and brains, a potent combination that had burned him before. Still, her resistance to the legend made Richard smile. "I could not agree more, Christina."

If only he could count on her resistance to a wedding. But once she realized a title and a kingdom accompanied the marriage vows, she would be singing a different tune.

"At least they agree on something." Alan grinned. "That's a good start."

"The ring does not fit," Richard said, feeling as though he had to keep repeating the phrase over and over again in order for the others to comprehend it.

Marguerite waved his words aside. "The ring has chosen Christina."

"No, Mother. It is stuck."

Christina nodded her agreement.

"Children, children. Don't you see? It's supposed to fit that way," Marguerite explained. "The ring is not stuck. Once you fall in love, it will come off. You must wed."

Christina looked like a butterfly caught in a net. Would she manage to escape unharmed? Would he? She stared at her father. "How can I marry him, Daddy?"

"You simply say 'I do,' sweetheart."

"No." Score one for the butterfly. "I can't."

"You can." Alan gave her shoulder a gentle squeeze. "And you will."

"But..." She hesitated. "I don't even *like* him."

Everyone in the room laughed; everyone in the room smiled. Everyone, that is, except Christina and Richard.

Sitting on the rock-hard, brocade-covered armchair, Christina felt as if she were waiting for Mozart to play his newest composition for a royal audience. Too bad what she was only waiting for was Prince Richard to say whatever it was he needed to say.

Though her floral-print cotton sundress felt out of place in the opulent music room, it was better than running around in his pajama top. Thank goodness he had given her time to shower and dress. Yet given the look of disdain on his face, she didn't think her choice of clothing mattered much to him.

Prince Richard leaned against the grandest piano she'd ever seen. Through the bow of windows, rays of light streamed in surrounding his head like a halo. But the look in his eyes was far from angelic. She pretended not to notice how the deep blue lapis columns, separating the ivory damask-swagged windows, intensified the color of those eyes.

She didn't understand him. Just as she was starting to figure him out, he would do something to surprise her. Prime example—his toothpaste. She would have expected him to be a roll-from-the-bottom-never-squeeze-in-the-middle kind of a guy, but the mangled tube of toothpaste she'd found on the counter of his bathroom had made him seem more human. Now she wasn't so sure. The back-and-forth was giving her whiplash.

And now this...

With a morning's growth of whiskers, he looked ruggedly handsome, a contrast to the traditional navy pants and meticulously pressed white oxford shirt he wore. Too bad the only thing Prince Richard would wear on his head was a crown. Put a Stetson on his head, dirty him up a bit, and he could pass for a cowboy.

"Christina," he said. The determined—make that cocky—set of Prince Richard's chin gave him a regal air of confidence. "Did you mean what you said in the salon?"

Time to face the music. Straightening her posture, she clasped her gloved hands together. "I'm sorry if I offended you, Your Highness. I shouldn't have said I didn't like you since we've known each other for less than twenty-four hours. Most likely I'm indifferent to you.''

"Indifferent?'' He narrowed his lips. "Are you always so...?''

She nodded. "Usually I'm much worse, Your Highness.''

"Why does that not surprise me?'' He sighed. "You do realize the ring on your finger means nothing to me.''

"Really?''

He nodded.

"Thank goodness.'' She smiled. "For a moment, I thought we were going to have to get married.''

"You do not wish to marry me?''

"No, Your Highness.''

"Even if it meant you would become a princess?''

"Not even if it would make me a queen.''

As Prince Richard studied her, his forehead wrinkled. "Besides being indifferent, is there another reason why you do not wish to marry me?''

She'd wounded his pride. He might be a prince, but he was still a man. Christina hesitated. "There are lots of reasons.''

"Lots?'' The color of his eyes darkened to the shade of midnight. "Please, enlighten me.''

She blew out a breath. "Well, I hate the way the press criticizes me and says I don't measure up to the Armstrong tradition of excellence. My entire life I've been nothing but fodder for the paparazzi, and I'm tired of it. I want to live my life out of the watchful eye of the media. To do that, I need to live in obscurity and out of the spotlight. That isn't possible if one is married to royalty.''

"No, it is not,'' he admitted.

"And your other reasons?''

"Children.''

He frowned. "You do not want them?"

"I want a farmhouse, not a castle, full of them." And she wanted to shelter her children from the same scrutiny and expectations she grew up with. Little princes and princesses would be required to live a certain kind of life, behave in a certain manner, follow the proper protocol. Just like little heiresses. "I want to raise my family in the country, not a foreign country, on a farm or a ranch. In a place like Wyoming or Montana, with lots of open spaces and animals and clear, big skies. Where you can get dirty and play in the mud and no one will care. Where you can have lots of pets and not get in trouble with any city ordinances. And where you have neighbors you actually know and like."

"It sounds so...common."

She nodded. "That's why it's so appealing. When I get home, I plan to move out West."

"To Montana or Wyoming?"

"Or Texas. I want to live a completely normal life."

"That does not sound like a normal life in America," he said. "Have you ever been to a farm or a ranch?"

"Of course." She tucked a strand of hair behind her ear. "A dude ranch, but I've seen pictures and read about real ranches and, um, cowboys."

He cocked an eyebrow. "Cowboys?"

"It's not that I have to marry a cowboy. A farmer, a mechanic. Any number of professions would do, but not..."

"Not what?"

"Not someone with a high-powered, time-consuming job," she admitted. "You see, I want to marry a man whose family will be his first priority. A man who will spend time and play with our children. A man who will work the land and not spend his days commuting to work or taking extended business trips."

"Did your father travel when you were growing up?"

"All the time. He and Mother were always jetting off and leaving me with my nanny."

"So you do not want to marry me because your life would not be...ordinary?"

"That's part of it."

His eyes widened. "There is more?"

"Well, the biggest reason is I don't love you." She didn't want to be in a loveless marriage. She might want to believe in the legend and the magical love spell, but for once in her life she had to be realistic. Prince Richard might be gorgeous and make her heart go pitter-pat every now and again, but she didn't love him. "I could never marry a man I didn't love."

He stared at her. "Do you know how many women would change places with you in an instant?"

His arrogance was showing again. Darn. She had hoped that part of his less-than-stellar personality had been due to tiredness. Oh, well. "Millions, Your Highness?"

"Yes, I..." He glanced at the ivory keys on the piano. "Perhaps not that many, but quite a few."

She bit back a grin. "You don't want to marry me, do you, Your Highness?"

"No."

"Why?" She chuckled at his shocked expression. "You don't have to answer that."

"You answered my question. I shall answer yours."

Christina wasn't sure she wanted to hear his answer. No doubt he would have as many reasons as she had.

"I want to choose my own wife."

How romantic. Maybe a small piece of Prince Charming did live inside Prince Richard. She felt a sudden connection to him. Her heart rate quickened. "So you want to marry for love, Your Highness?"

"Love? No," he said. "If I married you, all San Montico

would believe the legend was true. They already hate any sort of change or progress and prefer hanging on to their old ways. Marrying because of the Legend of the Ring would be the final nail in the coffin. San Montico would become as archaic and outdated as the legend."

The tone of his voice told her how much he loved his country. "But what about love, Your Highness?"

"What about it? For centuries, royalty have married for better reasons than love. A person can be happy without love."

So much for a connection. Once again, he had dashed her hopes that a fairy-tale prince could really exist. Oh, well...

"At least we are agreed," he said. "No wedding."

"No wedding," she echoed.

Christina stared into his eyes. A woman could get lost in those pools of blue. But not her, she reminded herself and glanced away.

"The next seven days will be difficult for us, Christina," he explained. "Wedding preparations, public appearances, interviews with the press."

She swallowed the pumpkin-size lump lodged in her throat. Surely Cinderella never had to deal with this much. "I'd prefer not to do any interviews, but I can handle the rest."

"I will see what I can do." He searched the room as if to assure they were alone. "Getting the ring off will require the utmost secrecy."

"Yes, Your Highness."

He leaned toward her. "It will have to be done when others are not around."

"I understand, Your Highness."

"No one can know."

"Look, Your Highness," she said, fighting the urge to knock some sense into that ego-filled head of his, "I may not have blue blood running through my veins, but I'm not a peasant who spends her days picking up cow dung and feels challenged by the task. I get it."

His eyes widened, but only for a second. "Good. Here is what we need to do...."

Chapter Five

Richard led Christina deep into the palace, through the library and gallery, by the blue room, past the yellow room, beyond the red room, into the white room and down a hidden staircase. It would have been faster to use the tunnels, but he did not want her to know about the secret passageways. Only members of the royal family and the royal advisor were privy to that information. And no matter what his mother might believe, Christina Armstrong would never become a de Thierry.

"Is it much farther, Your Highness?"

"We shall be there shortly." She sounded out of breath, so Richard stopped. "Would you like to rest?"

"No thanks. The sooner we get there, the sooner the ring comes off my finger."

The expectant look in her eyes made him hesitate, but only for a moment. It was the complete sight of her that made him do a double take. He really had not noticed her. Until now. In her flowered sundress and white gloves, she reminded him of a young Grace Kelly. All that was missing was a hat.

What was he thinking?

Grace Kelly had married Prince Rainier and become a princess. She and Christina had nothing in common besides being American.

"Gaston will know how to remove the ring." If not, Richard would be looking for a new royal jeweler. He started walking.

Christina followed him. "Why didn't we come here last night?"

"Because I was trying to keep the ring a secret."

"Well, since it's no longer a secret—" she tugged on her gloves to keep them from falling off "—may I remove the gloves?"

"May I remove the gloves, *Your Highness,*" Richard corrected her. "And the answer is no."

She sighed. "You do realize we're not fooling anyone, *Your Highness.*"

"Yes, but I prefer that the ring remain out of sight." He saw that the gloves were too large. "I shall get you a pair that fits."

They arrived at the end of the long passageway. Richard opened the heavy walnut-carved doors, then punched in the code to open the steel-vaulted doors.

"What is this place, Your Highness?"

"The royal jeweler's workshop."

"For a minute, I thought I was in a movie, and we were about to break into a bank." She grinned. "This place is more secure than Fort Knox."

Richard smiled at her wide-eyed awe. "The royal jewels must be kept safe."

"You must sleep well knowing they are so protected." As she walked past him into the windowless room, her dress swayed with the seductive motion of her hips. Her strappy sandals accented her long legs and delicate ankles.

He should not be noticing such things, Richard reminded himself.

She walked to a large rectangular table with microscopes on it and picked up a small metal container. "Look." She held a pearl up to the overhead light. "It's absolutely perfect."

He glanced at the open containers of gemstones, small gold bars, clasps and chains in gold, silver and platinum in every shape, size and length. "I would be careful if I—"

Christina hit her foot against a table leg and stumbled. She managed to keep herself balanced, but the pearls went flying. The metal container fell, clattering against the stone floor. The pearls rolled everywhere.

"Oh, no." She cringed and dropped to the floor, crawling after the pearls. "I'm so sorry, Your Highness."

He knelt, helping her retrieve the wayward pearls. "How old are you, Christina?"

"Twenty-four."

"Have you always been so...?"

"Klutzy? Accident-prone?" she offered. "Yes. For as long as I can remember. I don't do well in confined spaces and if I get nervous, it's even worse."

He froze, then looked at her. "Do I make you nervous, Christina?"

The corners of her mouth turned up slightly. "I'm afraid so, Your Highness. I'd watch out if I were you."

That was warning enough for him. "Stop what you are doing."

"But the pearls—"

"I will find the pearls." He pointed to a chair. "Sit. Do not touch anything."

Nodding, she took a seat.

Unbelievable. She was not only a menace to herself, but with all she came in contact. He was curious how her parents kept her under control. Did they lock her in a padded room?

After picking up the remaining pearls, he placed the full container on the table and sat in the chair next to her. "What do you do all day?"

"I work."

"You work?"

Her eyes narrowed. "This isn't the Stone Age. Women are allowed to work, Your Highness. At least, they are where I come from."

He tried to imagine what career she might have chosen. She had a natural talent for demolition. No doubt she could single- handedly overthrow a third-world country. "What type of work do you do?"

"I'm an artist, Your Highness."

"And what type of art do you create?"

Christina raised her chin. "I paint pet portraits."

"Pet portraits?"

She nodded. "Dogs, cats, hamsters, horses, snakes. You name it. I once painted a tarantula. I have the greatest job in the world."

"How did you decide to paint...pets?"

"I was going to be a veterinarian, but I couldn't stand to see animals in pain. I'd always loved to paint, so I combined my interests and *voilà*—a career I love."

Before Richard could respond, the royal jeweler, Gaston Carpentier, walked in. He placed his black leather medical bag on the worktable. "Pardon me for keeping you waiting, Your Highness."

Richard rose. "You must remove the ring from Miss Armstrong's finger at once."

"I shall try, Your Highness." Gaston tipped his hat at Christina. "Good day, *mademoiselle*. May I please see the ring?"

She glanced at Richard, and he gave her a nod to go

ahead. She removed her left glove and held out her hand for inspection.

Gaston placed a jeweler's loupe over his right eye. "What have you tried so far, Your Highness?"

"Lotions and oils."

"Vaseline and ice," Christina added.

Gaston studied her finger. "Hmmm."

What was taking so long? Richard wanted the ring off Christina's finger and the day over and done with. She could spend a few days at the beach, his treat, and he could get back to running his country. A perfect plan.

His hopes rested on the tall, lanky jeweler with a waxed mustache. Gaston opened his bag, pulled out a small glass jar and opened the lid. "This may work, Your Highness."

Richard stared at the pink concoction. "What is it?"

Gaston dipped two of his fingers into the jar and smothered Christina's finger with the thick substance. "A special formula."

She grinned. "It smells sweet, like candy."

"It is a secret recipe," Gaston explained. "Passed down through the generations of royal jewelers. I believe it was invented during the Renaissance."

Richard didn't care what its history was so long as it worked. "How long must we wait?"

"A few minutes, Your Highness." Gaston wiped his hands. "How do you like San Montico, Miss Armstrong?"

"San Montico is beautiful. I love the village with the cobblestoned roads and narrow streets. It's picture-postcard perfect. And the people are so polite and helpful. I got lost going to Astarte beach and a nice man helped me find my way."

"Astarte." Gaston sighed. "One of the unset gems of San Montico. But I thought Americans were not used to au naturel beaches."

Christina blushed. "No, but when in Rome..."

Gaston laughed. "Just remember your sunscreen."

Enough of the chitchat. Richard glanced at his watch. "Is it time?"

"Yes, Your Highness." Gaston blotted the excess formula from Christina's finger with a towel. He twisted the band, attempting to remove the ring. He tried again. "This is not promising, Your Highness."

"Let me try." Richard stepped between them. He pulled and tugged on the ring until tears welled in Christina's eyes. "It is still stuck."

"I do not understand." Gaston ran his fingers along his mustache. "My formula should have worked, Your Highness."

Richard jiggled the ring again. The band wouldn't budge. He wiped his hands. "We must try something else."

"Our alternative methods are somewhat...barbaric," Gaston said. "They may cause Miss Armstrong some pain."

Richard was not about to give up without pursuing every avenue. But he wasn't in this alone, and it wasn't his finger. "What did you have in mind?"

"We could wrap Christina's finger with wire or string or dental floss."

That did not sound too barbaric. Richard waited to see if Christina wanted to continue. She cleaned her hands with a damp cloth. "Go ahead."

Gaston hesitated. "It may hurt."

She extended her hand. "We don't seem to have too many other options at the moment."

"Such courage would be a strong trait in a princess," Gaston said under his breath as he rummaged through his bag and pulled out a coil of wire. "It's too bad the ring must come off."

Although Richard disagreed, he begrudgingly admitted he respected her tenacity. With her wealthy and privileged upbringing as part of America's corporate nobility, he expected her to be spoiled and selfish. Yet nothing about Christina had met his expectations. She had been understanding and selfless...even giving. Nothing like Thea, his ex-fiancée.

After winding the wire tightly around Christina's finger, Gaston tried once again to remove the ring. So did Richard. But the ring would not come off. So much for barbaric. He sighed.

Carefully, Christina unwrapped the wire. Gaston examined her swollen finger. "Would you like me to massage it or get a bag of ice?"

She flexed her fingers. "Don't worry. I'll be fine."

Too bad Richard was anything but fine. He would not be fine until the ring was off her finger. Something had to be done. "Cut it off."

Gaston gasped. "How could you suggest such a thing, Your Highness?"

"You can put it back together after it is off."

"Deplorable," Gaston said. "Do as you must, but I will not cut off Miss Armstrong's finger, Your Highness."

Christina clutched her left hand to her chest.

"Her finger?" Not even Richard was willing to do something so drastic. At least not yet. "I was talking about the ring."

"Oh, in that case..." A frown formed on Gaston's face. "The ring is irreplaceable. If something should go wrong, Your Highness..."

"Nothing will go wrong."

"But—"

"I take full responsibility." Richard searched Christina's face for a clue to her state of mind but found nothing to indicate any fear. "Christina?"

Her face paled, but she held her head high. "We must try, Your Highness."

"Proceed," he ordered.

Gaston pulled out a small electric handsaw and slid on a pair of protective goggles. "Are you positive you wish to…?"

Christina swallowed. "Yes."

"Keep your hand very still, *mademoiselle*." Sweat dotted Gaston's brow. "We will work slowly."

"It will be fine," Richard reassured her.

She chuckled. "Easy for you to say, Your Highness."

As her gaze focused on his, Richard felt himself drawing strength from the pair of emerald eyes staring into his. It should have been the other way around. Since his father's death, he had always been the rock, the one everyone leaned on. Yet Christina was here for him in a way he never could have imagined.

"For your protection, please look away, Miss Armstrong."

Christina turned and shielded her eyes with her right hand. Gaston powered up the saw. The spinning blade nicked the band with a shower of sparks. The grinding sound of the teeth replaced the whine of the saw. An instant later, the whirring of the blade stopped and two pieces of metal clattered onto the table.

Gaston stared at the pieces of blade. "It ripped in half."

"Try another," Richard instructed.

So Gaston did. The new blade split in two as the first had done. He tried again. The third blade spun off the tool and wedged itself in the stone floor. He tried yet again. The fourth blade's teeth melted away, leaving only a puff of smoke. Gaston turned off the saw, placed it on the table and removed his goggles. "It is futile, Your Highness. The magic spell protects the ring."

"There is no magic spell," Richard said. "Your blades are defective."

"All of them?" Christina questioned.

He ignored her. "Try something else."

"I have tried everything, Your Highness," Gaston explained. "The ring cannot be removed."

Richard's chest tightened. "There must be something you can do."

"I'm sorry, but there is nothing, Your Highness." Gaston closed his medicine bag. "I did my best, but there is no doubt."

"No doubt about what?"

"The Legend of the Ring, Your Highness." Gaston smiled. "It is true. The ring fits and only true love can remove it."

"True love." Christina fought the urge to sigh and quickened her steps to keep up with Prince Richard's long strides as he stormed through the palace. She understood why he was upset, but it wasn't as if the wedding were tomorrow. She wanted the ring off her finger, too, but it was cute how a grown man like Gaston could be so caught up in the wonder of the legend. Maybe it was something in the water. "You have to admit, Your Highness, it's kind of romantic."

"It is nothing of the sort." Prince Richard stopped in his tracks. "It is pitiful, nothing else."

"Gaston seemed to think—"

"Gaston is an imbecile. I should banish him from the island."

Christina planted her hands on her hips. "You'll do nothing of the sort. None of this is his fault. You promised to take full responsibility."

The sound of approaching footsteps stopped his reply. He looked around the room decorated in differing shades of red. "There are too many ears in the palace to discuss this here."

"You don't think people are spying on us, do you?"

"I would say the odds are very high that we are being watched," he whispered.

All this for a legend. It was so unbelievable. "Why, Your Highness?"

"So much is at stake, not only for us, but San Montico, too."

His gaze captured hers, and she experienced some magic of her own. Just as she was trying to understand the sudden feeling of butterflies in her stomach, the regal Princess Marguerite appeared at the doorway. Dressed in a black pantsuit with shiny gold buttons, she swept into the room. Christina could almost hear the strains of trumpets announcing the princess's arrival. An air of elegance and style surrounded her—the epitome of royalty and grace.

"Richard, Christina," Princess Marguerite greeted them. "I've been looking everywhere for you. There are a few wedding details we need to discuss."

"Later, Mother." Prince Richard took hold of Christina's elbow. "Let's go."

He hurried her into a room with drapes, rugs and furnishings the color of sunshine and lemons. The only things not yellow were Delia and her staff of designers. "Oh, Christina, here you are. We need to get a few more measurements."

"Not now, please." Christina grabbed Prince Richard's arm and pulled him through the doorway on the opposite wall into a room decorated in blues—cerulean, Dresden, navy, Venetian and Wedgwood. "That was a close call, Your Highness."

"Too close."

The marquess burst into the room. "Children, you won't believe my happy news." He clapped his hands together. "Doves. I found doves."

What should they do now? Christina looked at Prince Richard. He grabbed her hand. "Run." Like two naughty children escaping a scolding, they ran hand in hand out a pair of French doors to a flagstone walkway. A hundred yards down the path, Prince Richard stopped and let go of her hand. "Do you think we eluded them?"

Catching her breath, Christina glanced back. "I don't see anyone."

"Give them a minute."

"The only person missing was my father," she said. "I thought we'd find him waiting for us outside, but knowing him, I expect he's chartering the Concorde to fly wedding guests in."

Prince Richard's eyes widened. "He would not do such a thing."

"He would."

"This is so…"

"Appalling," she offered.

"Dreadful."

"Horrible."

He grinned. "Insane."

She started laughing, and Prince Richard joined in. Insane was right, but it was hard to take the situation too seriously. Especially with the marquess's announcement about doves. Thank goodness her mother wasn't here. That would push them right over the edge.

Christina wiped a tear from the corner of her eye. "What are we going to do, Your Highness?"

"I wish I knew," he said. "I do know we do not want to return to the palace. I would suggest a sail, but we would never make it to the marina with all the press lying in wait." He rubbed the stubble on his chin. "I know a place where we can escape all this for a little while."

"Are you sure? *They* seem to know our every move."

He smiled. "I promise you, they do not know this one."

Prince Richard led her along the path until they came to a wall of impenetrable green. A maze. The entrance, an arched lattice, was covered with bougainvillea. The bright pink flowers contrasted with the dark green of the manicured hedges lining the maze.

Christina plucked one of the small blossoms and tucked it behind her ear. "It's hard to believe all this madness is because of a legend."

"The legend is ingrained in the minds and the hearts of my people. That is why our marriage would only reaffirm their beliefs in the old ways of custom and tradition."

She could see his point, but traditions were what made each country, every culture, unique. Nothing was wrong with that. And what if by some wondrous means the legend were true. What then? "You don't think...?"

Richard stopped. "Are you starting to believe in...it?"

"No, of course not." She glanced up, and a pair of doves flew overhead. The marquess? Or magic? "But don't you think it was strange how none of the blades worked?"

"Coincidence."

"Let's hope," Christina said, but the words didn't sound as convincing as she would like.

Prince Richard gave her a funny look before leading her through the maze entrance. "There are no ears or eyes to escape from here. This is one of the most private spots on the palace grounds."

"Next to your bedroom?"

He smiled. "I prefer to be here during daylight hours."

Lucky for her. His bedroom was too intimate a place to hide. "Do you come here often, Your Highness?"

"Not often enough."

She stepped through the arch and stared at the five paths before her. So many choices. "Which way to the center?"

"You try to find it."

She took the rightmost path, and he followed her. "Did you play here when you were a child?"

"Yes. Didi and I would spend our days here. The chef

would stand by the entrance with chocolate crepes to lure us out. How did you guess?''

She pointed to the ten-foot walls of leaves. Braids of branches entwined, so thick the other trails were hidden from view. "It's the perfect place to play and hide."

Prince Richard smiled. "This was my special place. No one but Didi was allowed in."

"Not even your parents?"

"No one. Except the gardeners."

"It must have been nice. When I got in trouble, I usually hid in my grandfather's closet or under his bed."

"You were close to your grandfather?"

She nodded, wishing he were here now. Sometimes memories weren't enough. Especially when she needed advice or a hug. Like now. "Grandfather Armstrong moved in when I was seven and lived with us until he died five years ago. He always pretended not to care about anyone and acted all stiff and stuffy, but inside he was a big softy. He had pet nicknames for my cousins and me."

"What was yours?"

"I, um, it was just a silly little name." The name had meant the world to Christina, but she wasn't about to tell Prince Richard her nickname had been Princess. They were finally getting along, and she didn't want to spoil it. Time to change the subject. "So did the ring bring your parents together?"

"Unfortunately."

Christina turned a corner. The path ended at a small garden of topiary animals that put the ones at Disneyland's It's a Small World ride to shame. "Weren't they happy?"

"Deliriously happy. It was almost infectious." Prince Richard smiled. "They had the ultimate storybook love and marriage."

"That doesn't sound so bad." She approached a unicorn,

touched its horn for luck and headed back on the path. "What happened?"

He frowned. "My father died ten years ago, and all my mother has done since then is mourn. She is so young. She could remarry. Instead, she spends most of her time tending her garden and her charities."

"Isn't that her choice?"

"Yes, but..." Prince Richard brushed his hand through his hair. "She has put her total faith in the Legend of the Ring because it allowed her to find true love with my father. I cannot convince her that it is impossible for a ring or any inanimate object to bring love and happiness to a person. No matter what I say, she refuses to believe me."

The legend seemed to have so much power. Was there something to it?

He sighed. "If only I had married..."

Christina spun around and walked backward. "Would it have made a difference, Your Highness?"

"The legend applies only to unmarried princes." He caught her shoulder, preventing her from walking into one of the walls. "Be careful."

She would have to be careful. His touch was burning her skin. Burning in a feels-much-too-good way. Facing forward, she broke the contact. She reached a fork and took the left path. "So why haven't you married?"

"It is not for lack of trying, Christina, believe me. I have spent the past five years searching for a wife. But my pursuit... It has not turned out as I expected."

"I don't get it," she admitted. "You're a handsome prince. Every woman in the world is falling at your feet."

He raised an eyebrow. "Are you?"

She blushed. "Of course not, but you know why."

"Ah, yes." He smiled, complete with dimple. "The mythical cowboy."

It was no more a myth than Prince Charming. Okay, so

maybe both were myths. "I still can't believe you couldn't find a woman to marry."

The smile disappeared from his lips. "You really do not read the newspapers, do you?"

"No."

"Six months ago, I was engaged to an American like yourself. Her name was Thea—"

"Not Thea Hollis-Montgomery?"

"Yes. Why?"

Christina wasn't sure how to proceed. "I, um, know her."

His eyes narrowed. "How?"

"She was a sorority sister of my cousin Kelsey." Christina remembered the tall, leggy blonde with the alabaster complexion and a daddy who gave her everything, and anyone, she wanted. "Didn't she marry King Gus something or other a couple of months ago?"

Prince Richard nodded.

Realizing what must have happened sent Christina's mouth gaping. "She dumped you for a king?"

"You do have a way with words."

"I'm so sorry, Your Highness."

"Do not be sorry. It was for the best."

"Well, I always thought she was lacking in the brain-cell department, and her actions tell me I was right."

"Thank you, Christina."

"You're welcome, Your Highness."

"But she left me in quite a spot. Six months until my thirtieth birthday, until my deadline to wed."

And a broken heart, too. Poor guy—make that poor prince. No wonder he wanted nothing to do with the Legend of the Ring. "I can imagine how you've spent the past six months."

"You do not know the half of it," he admitted.

And she realized she didn't. Christina had never been in

love before, not real love, the kind-that-lasts-forever love. But one of these days…

Reaching the center, she climbed a short flight of stone steps to the top of a platform and looked down at the maze surrounding them. Beyond the palace grounds she saw the quaint village and the Mediterranean Sea that stretched to the horizon. It was all she could do not to ooh and aah over the sight. She glanced at the prince, who was watching her curiously. "What?"

"Do you like it?"

"It's incredible." She smiled. "You're so lucky to live here."

"Yes, I am." He paused. "You really could not make do with a palace and an entire kingdom as your…ranch?"

"No." It was tempting until she remembered all that came with it, and all that didn't, too. She looked away. "I'd probably set fire to it."

"Like the White House?"

Her jaw dropped. "You know about that?"

He nodded. "But not any of the details."

"You make it sound so sordid."

He cocked a brow. "Was it?"

"No, not at all."

"Care to elaborate?"

Christina hesitated. She did have the royal engagement ring stuck on her finger. It couldn't get much worse than that. And Richard had told her about Thea. Tit for tat. Besides, Christina had nothing to lose in telling something that had been reported by all the media and embellished in the tabloids. As her father always said, "At least they spelled your name correctly."

"Last Christmas, the president—he's a good friend of my father—was having a holiday get-together to trim one of his trees. The lights went out, so I grabbed a candelabra from the dessert buffet and brought it closer to the tree."

She wet her lips. "We stood around the tree and sang Christmas carols by candlelight. We were in the middle of 'Angels We Have Heard On High'—I love that one—when I got a little carried away with my 'Gloria' chorus. I guess I wasn't paying attention to the candelabra I was holding— I think I closed my eyes—because I set the president's cousin's hair on fire."

She expected Prince Richard to gasp or express his distaste at the incident, but he laughed instead. "I can imagine what happened next."

"I don't know about that." It was funny how the situation was almost humorous now, but then... "My grandfather always told me to join in when people laughed at something I did. He said it was better to laugh with people than to be laughed at. But no one was laughing that night.

"In my rush to help the president's cousin, I set the candelabra on the floor next to the Christmas tree. It must have been dry because it went up like a torch. Luckily, they managed to get the fire out before it did too much damage."

"And the cousin?"

"She was fine," Christina said. "Turns out she was wearing a wig with way too much hair spray on it."

"A party to remember."

"I'll always remember it. I'm sure everyone else will, too."

She chuckled. "Not exactly princess material, wouldn't you say, Your Highness?"

He shrugged. "I am not exactly cowboy material, either."

"No, you're not," she admitted, then grinned. "But you do have a few redeeming qualities. At times."

"So do you." That dimple of his seemed to wink at her, and her heart danced a little jig. "At times."

Chapter Six

Not cowboy material? What had made him say that? Being with Christina was turning his world upside down.

Giving her compliments, however true, might make her think he was having a change of heart. Of course, he wasn't. Not at all. He had just gotten caught up in the moment, in the race to escape the whirlwind of insanity sweeping the palace.

Christina might be nice, and he'd had more fun with her this afternoon than he'd had in the past six months, but nothing had changed between them. He did not want to share in the comfortable comraderie; he did not want to get to know her. He wanted only for her to leave his island. None of this was her fault, but she was the one who wore his ring. She was the one who threatened not only his throne, but his future and that of his country. Yet...

He had treated her as if she were a friend. Plotting to remove the ring, taking her to his maze, laughing with her. But she was not his friend. An ally, perhaps, but she would never be his friend.

And now he would have to survive a dinner discussion centering around the wedding, the reception and the honeymoon. No doubt his mother had the entire evening planned down to the last place card.

Richard entered the dining room and froze. The table was set with the finest china and crystal, which he expected, but seeing only two place settings took him by surprise, and that was not all. Burning candles, freshly cut flowers and a chamber orchestra setting up in the far corner of the room. His mother's signature was on everything.

It would not do. Not at all.

But he was not about to throw in his hand.

Two could play at this game.

First things first. He had to protect the palace. Nothing inflammable was nearby, but he was not taking any chances. He strode to the table and blew out the candles. Extinguishing the flames would not only keep any "accidents" from occurring but douse the romantic atmosphere suffocating the room. Now to take care of the musicians.

A short and pudgy violinist bowed. "Good evening, Your Highness."

"Thank you for coming, but your services are not necessary tonight."

"If you fear we will be intrusive, Your Highness," the cellist said, "we will play softly and be practically invisible."

The viola player smiled. "We understand your desire for a romantic dinner for two."

"Out," Richard ordered. "Before Miss Armstrong arrives."

"Yes, Your Highness," they said in unison. The musicians fell over themselves to pack up and get out of the dining room.

Richard rested his elbow against the mantel of one of the twin fireplaces and stared at the dancing flames. He had taken care of the most visible signs of his mother's match-making. He only wondered what else she had up her sleeve. If Richard knew her the way he thought he did, another long evening was ahead of him.

As Christina approached the dining room, she straight-ened her gloves. All day long she had struggled to keep them from falling off. Although she wasn't sure whether to wear them to dinner or not, Christina decided discretion was the better part of valor. After all, Prince Richard had asked her to wear them, and he was turning out to be a pretty decent guy, not the royal ogre she had glimpsed last night.

Christina stopped just outside the dining room. She glanced up, and her breath caught in her throat. Prince Richard leaned against the doorway. He'd shaved. Smooth skin replaced his whiskers. His damp hair was brushed back off his face, too. Gorgeous, absolutely gorgeous. But still a prince, she reminded herself. No matter how much she might have felt like his partner in crime today, it didn't change the facts. A royal wedding would not be taking place. She didn't want to marry him; he didn't want to marry her.

He held out his hand, and she stepped toward him. The heel of her black leather pump caught on the carpet. Her ankle twisted, but she miraculously maintained her balance. Maybe the ring did possess some magic powers; otherwise she'd be spread-eagled on the floor.

Prince Richard bowed. "Christina."

She caught a whiff of the woodsy scent of his soap, and her pulse sped up. She curtsied. "Your Highness."

"How do you like your rooms?"

She had been moved to a suite across the hall from his. "It's lovely. Thank you."

He stared at her hands. "Your gloves, please."

Had she made a fashion faux pas by wearing them to the dining room? She bit the inside of her cheek. That's all she needed—to be the "Don't" picture at the back of *Glamour* magazine. Christina removed the gloves and gave them to him.

He pulled another pair from his shirt pocket and handed them to her. "These should fit better."

She couldn't believe he'd remembered after everything they had been through today. She tried them on—a perfect fit. "Thank you, Your Highness."

He motioned her into the dining room. Thank goodness Prince Richard wasn't wearing a suit or tuxedo. Even though he wore pleated black pants, a starched white dress shirt and a colorful silk tie, Christina felt underdressed. Whoever said a little black dress could go everywhere had never stepped into the formal dining room of San Montico Palace.

As large as her entire apartment in Chicago, the dining room had twin marble fireplaces at either end. Red damask fabric covered the walls; a matching rug covered the parquet hardwood floor. Two giant gilt chandeliers hung overhead.

Dominating the room was a long, rectangular table that could seat at least thirty distinguished guests, but it looked bare with one place setting at the head and another around the corner to its right.

Only two? She gulped.

"It appears we will be dining alone."

Alone? She wasn't sure that was a good or a bad thing. The wedding talk would be kept to a minimum, but what else might happen with only the two of them there? More time alone with him would be dangerous to her hormones. Thank goodness her heart was immune. "Where is everyone?"

"I fear we have been set up." He motioned to a candelabra with unlit candles, a bottle of champagne chilling on ice, fires crackling in the fireplaces and a fresh bouquet of flowers in a cut-crystal vase. "My family is trying to set the stage for a little romance."

A *little* romance? Understatement of the year. Pretend the other twenty-eight chairs weren't there and this could easily qualify as one of the top ten romantic places to kiss in the world. Not that she wanted a kiss. Okay, maybe just one. A little one.

"Would you prefer to eat elsewhere?"

Christina was afraid where elsewhere might be. She looked at Prince Richard, who had pulled out a chair, then hurried to her seat. "No, Your Highness, this is fine."

Sitting at the head of the table, Richard rang a silver bell with an ornately decorated handle. Two uniformed waiters entered the dining room through a door. One waiter lit the candles; the other filled her water goblet and poured the champagne.

That still left several crystal goblets empty—Chardonnay, Merlot, Cabernet Sauvignon, Pouilly-Fuissé, Chablis, Bordeaux, Riesling, Burgundy, Pinot Noir, zinfadel and port? Why not toss in Asti Spumante, Chianti and retsina? She didn't know the names of enough wines to fill all the glasses.

Not to mention all the silverware in front of her. Christina had been raised properly and knew what utensil to use when and how to position her knife and fork when pausing or finishing a meal, but with the spread in front of her she could easily make a mistake and send Letitia Baldrige, Miss Manners and Emily Post into histrionics if proper etiquette allowed for such a reaction.

Another waiter carried in two small plates. "Homemade game pâté in Madeira aspic, Your Highness."

"Thank you, Jean-Claude."

Jean-Claude set the plate in front of her. Christina stared at the pâté, but didn't touch it.

Prince Richard stared at her. "Are you not hungry?"

Actually, she was starved. Both breakfast and lunch had been forgotten in the attempt to remove the ring, but that had given her an idea about how to get it off. "A little."

"If you do not like pâté, I can have the chef prepare something else."

"That isn't necessary. It's just. . ."

"What?"

She glanced around to make sure the waiters were gone. "I thought if I lost some weight, the ring might come off."

His lips narrowed. "You will stop this line of thinking at once."

"We're running out of options, Your Highness."

"Endangering your health is not the way to get the ring off." He picked up his flute of champagne. "I forbid it."

"But—"

"It is not open for discussion, Christina."

Not open for discussion? Who did he think...? She saw him watching her. When she met his gaze, he looked away nonchalantly and blew out the candles, but not before she glimpsed what his eyes could not hide.

He cares whether I eat or not.

His concern filled her with a warmth so comforting she wanted to give him a great big bear hug and say thank-you. She wanted to forget he was "Your Highness" and call him "Richard." But Christina wasn't in a position to do such a thing no matter how good her intentions, so she ate a bite of the pâté instead.

Silver scraped and clinked delicately against the china. She waited for Prince Richard to say something, anything, but he didn't. Instead, he took exact bites of his appetizer, measured sips of his water. Their earlier rapport had vanished, to be replaced with an uncomfortable silence. Was it against protocol to talk during meals? She didn't know, and it was driving her crazy. What she could really use was a shot of tequila. Of course, that would be the only glass missing.

Jean-Claude reentered, relit the candles on the table and scooped up the empty appetizer plates. Another waiter brought in bowls. "Consommé Millé Fanti with egg drops and flavored with sherry, Your Highness."

"Thank you, Jacques."

Jacques placed the steaming bowl in front of her. Christina was not going to let the only sound in the room be her slurping the soup. Forget it. "It's really quiet in here, Your Highness."

Prince Richard held his spoon in midair. "Would you like music? I can summon a chamber orchestra."

A bit much on such short notice. She'd been thinking along the lines of dropping a CD in the stereo. "No need for that, Your Highness, but a little conversation might be nice."

Swallowing a spoonful of her soup, she tasted the sherry in the broth. A bit strong, but maybe this was how royalty liked their food. Jacques smiled at her and left the room.

Prince Richard leaned toward her. "They are trying to get us drunk."

"I was wondering why the broth tasted so...strong." She set her spoon down. "They really expect us to marry, don't they?"

He nodded. "The sooner, the better. And if we happened to get caught in a compromising situation...our fate would be sealed."

"This is so...unreal."

He glanced at the closed door she assumed led to the kitchen. "We must not play into their hands, Christina. We must not let them think they are succeeding."

Success would mean marriage. Something neither of them wanted.

Jacques returned with a bottle of red wine. He poured a taste for Prince Richard, who nodded his approval.

Wine? She didn't want a glass. She wanted only to show the hovering waiters their scheme was not working, but how? Christina struggled to find the right words, safe words, to say. "Does San Montico always have such nice weather, Your Highness?"

Prince Richard patted his mouth with a napkin. "Yes, though we do get an occasional rain shower."

"I like taking walks in the rain."

"I like walks in the rain, too." Sipping his wine, Prince Richard watched Jacques leave the dining room, then blew out the candles. "Tomorrow morning, we will seek the advice of a wizard."

Why not follow the yellow brick road? "You don't believe in magic," she reminded him.

Richard smiled. "This wizard does not practice real magic."

"But what do we do about tonight?"

He motioned to the door where Jacques was surreptitiously sticking his head out. As soon as the waiter realized he'd been caught, he disappeared behind the closed door. Richard's eyes twinkled mischievously. "I say we continue an enlightened discussion about the weather for our audience."

Christina could imagine him as a little boy hiding in the maze. She grinned. "That's too cruel."

"No, cruel is my mother's not-so-subtle flower arrangement." He motioned to the bouquet on the table. "See the white roses?"

Their light fragrance mixed deliciously with the aroma of the food. She stared at the velvety white petals. "They are beautiful."

"Yes, but my mother has been growing these especially for my wedding. She says it's a tradition for the de Thierry bride to carry three white roses in her bouquet."

"Why three?"

"One for the groom, one for the bride and one for San Montico."

How romantic. Wait a minute. Three in a marriage. Why not add a fourth for the paparazzi? "Sounds like the de Thierrys share one crowded marriage bed."

"It can—"

The entrance of Jean-Claude and Jacques interrupted the prince. "The low pressure fronts cause thunderstorms. Not the high pressure fronts, though those can cause their own problems." Christina tried not to smile at the confused look exchanged by the two waiters. "Does that clear up your question, Your Highness?"

Jacques refilled their glasses and relit the candles. Jean-Claude set a crystal goblet of sorbet in front of her. The peach sorbet melted in Christina's mouth. Sweet and refreshing. Just what she needed to cleanse her palate.

Prince Richard drew his eyebrows together, then nodded. "And you are certain about this phenomenon?"

The two waiters frowned. She bit back a smile. "Quite sure. I took a meteorology class in college. We studied this in depth."

"How fascinating."

About as fascinating as watching golf on television. Christina took another bite of sorbet, then set her small spoon down. As soon as she did, Jean-Claude carried the goblets to the kitchen, and Jacques followed.

Richard blew out the candles again, then laughed. The deep, rich sound made her feel all tingly inside. She chalked it up to the romantic atmosphere of the evening. "I do believe they think I have lost my mind. Talking to a beautiful woman about something as boring as weather patterns. You were wonderful.''

Wonderful? She was still stuck on his calling her beautiful. ''Do you think we fooled them?''

''Completely. Wait until my family hears.'' He smiled, one of those wide, Prince Charming smiles that set her heart aflutter. ''My uncle considers himself an expert on women. I have no doubt he will tutor me on how to woo and court you properly.''

Not that Richard—make that *Prince* Richard—needed any help. If he wanted to, he could win a woman with his smile alone. Not that he wanted to win her. He didn't. And she didn't want to be won. But sitting here, conspiring against the matchmaking, made it easy to forget she wanted nothing to do with him.

Nothing, nada, zilch.

Just as he wanted nothing to do with her.

She smiled at him; he smiled back, dimple and all. Her tummy tightened and did what felt like a handspring with a half twist. Must be the champagne, she rationalized, and reached for her goblet of water.

Jean-Claude brought in the entrées. He frowned when he noticed the snuffed-out candles. ''Roast duckling a l'orange, Your Highness.''

Prince Richard nodded.

Jean-Claude set a plate in front of her. Duck, orange slices, broccoli, red cabbage and croquette potatoes. ''Smells delicious. Please give my compliments to the chef.''

''I will tell him, *mademoiselle*.'' Jean-Claude smiled. ''He used a Grand Marnier sauce on the duck. Our chef takes extra care with his special dinners.''

Prince Richard cleared his throat. ''What about hurricanes? I have never quite understood how they spin in one direction in the Northern hemisphere and rotate in the opposite direction in the Southern hemisphere.''

"Oh, yes." Christina smiled her most charming smile. "Now that's really interesting, Your Highness."

Richard leaned close and stared at her, utterly fascinated. "Please, tell me more."

Following dinner, Prince Richard accompanied her upstairs. "Now, that is what I call stimulating dinner conversation."

Poor Jacques and Jean-Claude had been beside themselves over the weather discussion. Every time the waiters refilled the water goblets, they had stared at the full wineglasses with such despair, and they couldn't understand why the candles kept needing to be lit. No doubt they hadn't heard about the incident at the White House. Christina chuckled. "Yes, but I feel sorry for them."

Prince Richard laughed. "They gave it their best try, did they not?"

"Yes." None of the waiters' obvious attempts to change the direction of the conversation or serve more alcohol had worked, much to their dismay. "But you wouldn't budge an inch."

"No." He stopped in front of the door to her room. "Did you really take a meteorology class?"

Fooled even him. "No, but I've watched the weather channel. Cable is a wonderful thing."

His gaze met hers. "We were quite the team."

Her pulse picked up speed. "Yes, we are, I mean, were."

"I enjoyed tonight, Christina."

So had she. "It was…fun."

He leaned toward her and tucked a stray lock of hair behind her ear. "Yes, it was fun."

He sure smelled good. Be careful. "I, uh, guess I should say good-night."

"Allow me." He reached for the door handle.

If he kept smiling like that, she would allow him to do whatever he... No, she wouldn't. She needed to get away from him. Now. Christina reached for the door handle, too, and her hand covered his.

Warm.

The feel of his skin against her palm made her suck in a breath. Her heart pounded. She hoped he would kiss her good-night; she wanted him to kiss her good-night.

No, she didn't. He wasn't just a man. He was a prince. P-R-I-N-C-E. She jerked her hand away.

He opened the door to her room, then lifted her chin with his fingertips. "What are you afraid of?"

You. She gazed into his eyes. "Y-y-you have calluses."

He stared back. "From sailing."

"But you're a p-p-prince."

"Want to know a little secret? Royalty are not that different."

No? Larger than life was the only way to describe him. Prince Richard radiated confidence. Intelligence shone through his sparkling blue eyes. He commanded respect no matter what he did. He was so different from any man she'd ever met—a prince in every sense of the word.

She fought the urge to sigh. "How can you say that? You live in a magnificent palace on the top of a hill and rule over a beautiful kingdom."

"You have a president who lives in a big white house and rules over one of the most powerful nations in the world."

"It's not the same."

"No, it is not." He moved closer to her. "Have you ever kissed royalty, more specifically a prince, before?"

She took a step away and backed into the door frame. Her heart thudded. "No, I mean, I—"

He didn't give her time to finish. His mouth came down

on hers without a moment's hesitation. Just a brush of his lips. So full, so soft, so tender, so warm. His kiss teased, hinted of more to come. She wanted more, much more. But as quickly as he started the kiss, he ended it.

"So what do you think?" he asked with a sly look in his eyes.

Christina couldn't tell him the truth. She couldn't tell him his kiss—little more than a brush of his lips—had forever changed her definition of what a good kiss should be. She uncurled her toes. "You're right, Your Highness. Royalty aren't different from anyone else."

"Is that right?" he whispered.

Self-preservation had her nodding.

He laughed. "Good night, Christina."

"Thank you, Your Highness. For dinner and…everything."

Shut up, she told herself. Afraid if she looked at Prince Richard again she would invite him in, Christina retreated into her room. Clutching the inside handle for strength, she closed the door before he could say anything to make her change her mind.

Because she wanted him to say something so she would.

Richard closed the door to his bedroom and locked it. Not to keep anyone out, but to keep himself in. He could simply walk across the hall and wish Christina good-night again. No one would know.

Whom was he kidding? He did not want to say goodnight to Christina. He wanted to kiss her again. And not a chaste good-night peck. He wanted to—

A knock sounded at his door.

Christina. Smiling, he opened the door. "Did you forget…Uncle?"

"May I come in?"

As Richard opened the door wider, he fought the wave

of disappointment washing over him. He should not care whether Christina was at his door or not, and it bothered him that it did. "Come in, Uncle Phillippe."

The marquess entered and clasped his hands behind his back. "What is wrong with you?"

"Excuse me?"

"You spend a romantic dinner with a beautiful woman and discuss the weather?"

For such a large palace, word traveled fast. "We had a pleasant conversation."

Phillippe glanced at the ceiling. "Youth is wasted on the wrong people. Don't you understand, Richard? You have a responsibility, a duty to marry."

Richard knew it would come to this. "I shall marry, but not now."

"This isn't a whim or a fancy of your mother's. You must marry Christina."

"I shall marry the woman I choose."

"You had your chance."

"That is not fair, Uncle. You know I have done my best. I have dated more women than you and father combined. The press dubs me a playboy when all I want to do is find a wife."

"Since you didn't find one, perhaps the press is right."

"Even you were relieved when Thea and I broke up."

"Yes, we all were. But what about the supermodel?"

"That did not work out."

"Because she snored?"

Richard released an exasperated sigh. "I did not break up with *her* because she snored. She would not have been good for San Montico."

"Since when did San Montico start weighing in on your marriage decisions?"

"I have always considered San Montico's needs just as I have considered my own. It is not easy finding a woman who can be both a princess to my country and a wife to me. But once I find her, I will marry her. It shall be my choice, however.''

''If you do not choose to marry Christina, it will be bad for all of us.''

''Not for you.''

''I have never wished to rule.''

''You are only trying to force me into a corner.''

''No, Richard, I am not. I'm the third son. There was your father. And your uncle Etienne. God rest their souls.'' Phillippe made the sign of the cross. ''No one expected the throne to pass to me. Everyone, myself included, was so relieved when you were born.''

''What are you saying, Uncle?''

''I will not take the throne.''

The words almost knocked Richard over. It was like being hit by the boom of his sailboat on a mistimed jib. His ancestors had struggled over the centuries to retain the throne, the monarchy. Many had suffered unthinkable fates in the process—torture, war, starvation, death. San Montico was a part of his family, a part of him. ''Why?''

''I was not groomed to rule. It's something I've never wanted.'' Phillippe closed his eyes, then opened them slowly. ''If I were to take the throne, I would destroy all that our family has accomplished over the centuries. Remember the jubilee dinner I organized and the financial mess that followed?''

Richard nodded. Four years later, and the Royal Treasury was still paying off the cost overruns. ''Yes, but—''

''I accept my limitations. I was not born to be a leader.''

''Please, Uncle, you cannot be serious.''

''I am, Richard. God help us, but I am,'' Phillippe admitted. ''If you do not marry Christina, the rule of the de Thierrys will end.''

Chapter Seven

It was too early to be up. Stifling a yawn, Christina held her arm out to Prince Richard. With gentle hands, he wrapped an elastic bandage around her left hand and wrist. "How does that feel?"

Much too good. Those light caresses, the brush of his fingertips against her skin, were shooting sparks all the way up her arm, down her spine, straight to her belly and beyond. A few minutes more and a fire was going to ignite. She tried to pull away, but he held on to her hand. "It's fine, Your Highness."

He secured the wrap and ran his finger along the length of her bandaged arm. "Is it too tight?"

"No." Maybe if it were too tight, her circulation would keep the boiling blood from running through her entire body. She stared at her hand. "This is never going to work."

"No one will see us." Prince Richard handed her a pair of sunglasses. "The streets are deserted at this time in the morning. Most people are still in bed."

Both she and Prince Richard should be in bed, too. Their own beds, she amended. Last night's kiss had turned her into a swooning maiden. At least that was better than a swooning bride. She glanced at her "I'm with him" T-shirt. "We're going to be recognized."

"Anyone who sees us will think we are on our honeymoon." He placed a black baseball cap on his head. "Groom" was embroidered in white script on the front.

"If we were on our honeymoon, we wouldn't be up at the crack of dawn."

Prince Richard smiled. "Not necessarily."

The glint in his eyes suggested she let his remark pass without comment. She picked up her coordinating "Bride" baseball cap and placed it on her head. "Where did you find all this stuff?"

"My mother keeps a hope chest for me. It is full of matching hats and shirts for a newlywed couple to wear."

Under any other circumstances, Christina would have thought that sweet, but not when she was the intended bride.

Prince Richard picked up her sketchbook from a nearby writing desk and stared at it. "You are talented."

Last night, she had started working on a new drawing—a cowboy and his horse. The sketch was hardly defined, just a few strokes of her pencil so far, but she appreciated the compliment. "Thanks."

He set the pad down. "We must go."

"I have a funny feeling about this."

"There is no time for funny feelings." He covered his eyes with a pair of mirrored sunglasses. "Come."

A fruit truck was idling at the rear entrance to the palace. She and Prince Richard climbed in the back and covered themselves with a citrus smelling canvas tarp. It was cramped quarters, but when the truck pulled away she realized they'd made a successful escape.

The truck rounded a corner, and Christina collided against Prince Richard. As the truck swung in the opposite direction, his strong arms kept her from careering into the other side of the bed. His touch made her long for another kiss, but before she could contemplate it further, the truck stopped.

Prince Richard threw back the tarp and climbed out. He held out his arms to help her down. "Hurry."

He led her to a small alleyway. No one was out, but Prince Richard peeked around the corner before crossing the street. The morning light glinted off the sun-bleached ends of the hair sticking out of his hat. His "I'm with her" T-shirt stretched across his chest and arms, and his khaki shorts and tan, muscular legs set her imagination in motion.

He led her to a cottage. The plastered walls were cracked; the stones at the foundation covered with moss. Above the front door was a wooden sign that read Beware Ye Who Enter. Ye Might Not Like What The Future Holds.

The door opened before he could knock. A small man, whose long white hair stood on end, greeted them. "Please, come in."

Following Prince Richard's lead, she stepped inside. Drying herbs and flowers hung from the beamed ceiling and scented the air. Sage, lavender, rosemary. She couldn't name all the smells. Crystal stones and globes lined shelves on the stone walls and reflected the flickering light of candles illuminating the small interior. She stared at the little man with his electrified hair and ice-blue eyes. Wearing a flowing purple robe with a magenta satin cape, he was a cross between a mad scientist and a deranged wizard.

"I've been expecting you, Your Highness." The man bowed. "And you, too, Miss Armstrong."

He knew her name. Was he really a wizard? Clairvoyant? Christina glanced at Prince Richard, who stared at a crystal ball and deck of tarot cards on a velvet-covered table with a look of disbelief on his face. "How did you know we were coming?"

"The royal advisor called and told me to expect you."

Prince Richard nodded. "Of course he did."

The little man laughed. "I see from your expression, Your Highness, this is not what you expected."

With furrowed brow, Prince Richard released a drawn-out sigh. No doubt he was as confused about this place as she was. "It is not."

"Pay no attention to the surroundings, Your Highness. Just props for my new business venture. Fortunes and spells. Herbs and potions. A far cry from my former position as royal jeweler, but a man must earn a living."

Christina studied him. "*You* were the royal jeweler?"

He made a flourish with his cape. "Merlin at your service."

"We need your help," Prince Richard said.

"After all these years." The magician—make that ex-royal jeweler—placed his hands over his heart. "To have left the palace in such disgrace and to have you ask me, your humble servant, for help. You do me a great honor, Your Highness. A great honor indeed." Merlin stepped to the front of his tiny shop, locked the door and placed a Closed sign in his window. "How may I assist you, Your Highness?"

Prince Richard unwrapped the bandage, revealing the royal engagement ring. "Remove the ring from her finger, and I will reinstate you as royal jeweler."

Merlin's wide eyes filled with tears. "This is so much more than I could ever imagine. May I examine the ring, Your Highness?"

Prince Richard nodded, and she extended her arm. Merlin pulled out a magnifying glass from one of his many pockets. Touching the ring with reverence, he studied the ring's fit from different angles. His wrinkled hand felt cold against her skin. Finally, he looked up. "Did that idiot try the pink stuff—the royal jeweler's secret formula?"

"Yes," Prince Richard said. "But is that any way to speak of your brother?"

"Half brother, Your Highness," Merlin corrected respectfully. He gestured to a table at the far side of the room. "Please be seated. I shall return momentarily."

As Christina sat, he disappeared behind a curtain. "Merlin seems nice, but a bit...odd."

"He is a bit...eccentric, but desperate times call for desperate measures."

"We can't be that desperate, Your Highness. It's only Monday."

"Do not worry about Merlin. He was a fine jeweler...once."

Once? That wasn't the reassurance she wanted. "What happened? Or is it better I don't know?"

Prince Richard smiled. "I was only a child, but I remember he melted two pieces of irreplaceable heirlooms— the seal of Prince Alexander the Undefeated and Princess Katerina's betrothal bracelet. To hide his mistake, Merlin made a set of royal jacks for me. My father was furious. Merlin disappeared and was found wandering the streets wearing Princess Nicolette's diamond tiara from the crown jewel collection, one of my mother's silk caftans and a pair of her Ferragamos."

This was worse than she thought. Christina swallowed hard.

Carrying two glass vials in one hand, a leather-bound book in the other, Merlin returned and set everything on the table. He removed the lids from the gray vial and the green vial. "Any jeweler should know conventional methods will not work with an enchanted ring."

Prince Richard crossed his arms. "The ring is not enchanted."

"It is still on her finger. The only explanation is magic. We must fight the spell with one of our own."

Christina glanced at Prince Richard, who merely shrugged. Might as well see what happened.

From one vial, Merlin poured a shimmering pink powder onto his palm. From the other, he poured white sand. "Ready?"

Holding her breath, Christina extended her hand. Merlin released the powder over her finger. It sparkled and settled around the ring. He closed his eyes, raised his hands and muttered a dozen words in a language she'd never heard before.

"Try the ring now," Merlin urged in a whisper.

She tried but couldn't remove it. Neither could Prince Richard. Damn. She really wanted this to work. "What is this?"

"Fairy and pixie dust."

Prince Richard grimaced. "You have got to be kidding."

Merlin smiled. "I didn't think it would work, but I thought why not give it a try."

Hopeless. Her future rested with an odd little man who believed in magical dust. The ring was never going to come off. She would have to marry Prince Richard or cut off her finger. She wasn't sure which would be worse. Christina buried her head in her hands.

Prince Richard gave her shoulder a reassuring squeeze. "Do not give up."

His words made her sit straighter. This wasn't the time to overreact. She took a deep, calming breath. She would get through this; they would get through this. "What do we do now?"

Merlin's forehead wrinkled. "The ring has somehow

welded itself to the skin. Unless, of course, a man-made substance was—''

''I did not glue the ring to my finger,'' Christina said, offended.

''Then there is no doubt,'' Merlin announced. ''The ring fits, Your Highness. She is to be your wife.''

''I do not believe this.'' Prince Richard clenched his teeth. ''First Gaston. Now you.''

Merlin puckered his lips. ''Gaston couldn't remove a necklace from a giraffe. He is worthless, Your Highness.''

''You are no better,'' Prince Richard said.

''What to do, what to do?'' Merlin drummed his fingers on the table. ''You do not wish to marry Miss Armstrong, Your Highness?''

Prince Richard glanced at her, and her heart skipped a beat. ''I...I will not allow a legend to tell me whom to marry.''

''And you do not wish to marry him, Miss Armstrong?''

The scowl on Prince Richard's face made him look dangerous, but that made him even more attractive. ''I, er, I don't want to marry a prince.''

''Think, think, think.'' Merlin murmured the mantra with his eyes closed. Suddenly, he opened his eyes, stood and pushed an old book toward them. ''Read this. I will be back.''

Merlin vanished behind the curtain again. Christina blew the remaining fairy and pixie dust from her finger and covered Prince Richard's face with sparkling specks. He sneezed.

''Sorry, Your Highness.''

He brushed the glittering powder from his face.

A dab remained, shimmering on his nose. ''You, uh, missed a spot.'' As she wiped the pixie dust off, he stared at her. The edges of his mouth curled up—a devastating grin that hinted of things Christina could only dream about.

She felt drawn to him, but it made no sense. She couldn't be attracted to him; she couldn't be wanting to kiss him again. "What do we do now, Your Highness?"

Instead of fulfilling her dreams, he pointed to the title of the book: *The Legend of The Ring.* "We read this."

No reason to feel disappointed or rejected. *Remember, he's all wrong for you.* One kiss had been more than enough. She didn't want any more complications. She wet her dry lips.

As Prince Richard opened the book, the bindings cracked with age. The pages smelled musty, but what pages. Gold leafed with ornate, hand-drawn, colored borders. Such craftsmanship.

"This must be hundreds of years old." Christina stared in awe. Even the text, written in an elaborate script, was a work of art. "What does it say?"

"'The Legend of the Ring Throughout the Ages.'" He turned to page one and read aloud.

Halfway through the book, he stopped reading. Through the ages, generation after generation, the legend had proven true. In each case, the ring had fit and a royal marriage had occurred within a week, making their own situation bleaker. Christina took over reading.

"This is the last story." She began with the introduction, dating back to the 1600s. "'...and on the prince's thirtieth birthday, a servant from the palace kitchen, Patricia, joined the line of eligible women waiting to try on the royal engagement ring. When Patricia reached the front of the line, the prince's entourage laughed at her tattered clothes and bare feet. The royal advisor informed her that servants were not allowed to try on the ring. The news devastated Patricia, and she began to cry. You see, Patricia loved the prince with all her heart. She had loved him since childhood, from the first day she arrived with her parents and saw the prince riding his magnificent stallion on the palace grounds.'"

A lump formed in Christina's throat. She stopped reading.

"Is something wrong?"

Tears stung her eyes. She blinked several times. "No, it's just so sad. Can you imagine loving someone forever and not being able to do anything about it?"

"Not at the moment." Prince Richard smiled and caressed her cheek with his fingertip. "Do not let it upset you. With our luck, this story will have a happy ending, too."

She nodded, ignoring the thundering of her heart. His one little touch and...and she shouldn't be thinking about it. "'The prince saw the beautiful young woman and was touched by her tears. He decreed that all women, regardless of their station in life, would be allowed to try on the ring. The advisor apologized to Patricia. The prince wiped the tears from her face and placed the ring on her finger. A perfect fit.'"

Prince Richard blew out a puff of air. "I told you so."

Nodding, Christina read on. "'Three days before the royal wedding, the ring came...off.'"

This was it. Exactly what they were looking for. Her gaze caught Richard's, then she returned to the story.

"'The royal advisor declared the legend invalid. With the ring no longer on her finger, the wedding did not have to—'"

"How did the ring come off?" Richard leaned closer to her, his shoulder touching hers. The spicy scent of him made her nerve endings dance.

"Let me see." Searching for her spot, she ignored the feel of his muscular thigh pressing against hers. So warm. So hard. "Where was I? 'The ring,' no...that's not it. Here. 'The wedding did not have to take place. But the prince told his advisor he only removed the ring so he could propose properly. He loved Patricia and wanted to marry her. Legend or not.'''

"Damn."

Christina bit her lip. "I hate to say it, but it looks as if Didier was right. Only true love will remove the ring."

Before Prince Richard could say anything, Merlin burst into the room like cannon fire. "If I cannot remove the ring, but you are satisfied with whom you marry, will I get my position back?"

Prince Richard hesitated, but only for a moment. "Yes. So long as it is…legal."

"Wonderful, Your Highness." Merlin's grin spread ear to ear. "Because I have found a solution. Two, actually."

Merlin called this a solution?

Pacing back and forth, Richard ducked his head to keep from hitting the dead flowers hanging from the rafters. "I do not care what you say, Merlin. I am not going to fall in love with her."

Christina's lips narrowed. "Well, I'm not falling in love with him."

Merlin frowned. "Too bad I don't have the stories of modern times, including that of your parents, Your Highness. Then you would see."

Richard stopped pacing and clasped his hands behind his back. "They are nothing but fairy tales."

"How can you say that? You read the book. If you fall in love, the ring will come off. It's the easiest way. I could work up a love potion. I've never had much success with No. 9, but I've heard of wonderful results using No. 23 and No. 30."

"No," he and Christina shouted in unison.

"Children, children." Merlin massaged his temples. "That leaves my other solution."

"I would not call it a solution." Richard had been

searching for a wife, but he had always believed the ring would not fit anyone. He had always had that as an out. Until now. "Given time, we would have thought of it ourselves."

Merlin crossed his arms in front of his chest and stuck out his lower lip like a pouting child. "But I thought of it first, Your Highness."

"Yes, you did." Which meant Richard would not only have to resume his search and scour the globe for a bride, but he would also have to keep his word and reinstate Merlin as the royal jeweler. If his solution worked. Richard would also have to keep Gaston. Having the two half brothers work together would be difficult, but Gaston's presence was the only way to protect the royal jewels from Merlin's eccentric nature. "However, it could add more complications."

"Minor complications, perhaps," Merlin admitted. "But the choice will be yours, Your Highness. That is what you want."

It would let him keep his throne and choose his own wife—well, sort of choose her. "Yes, but—"

"It will solve everything, Your Highness." Christina rose from the table. "Of course, we'll still have to figure out how to get the ring off my finger, but at least you keep your throne."

The time constraints and the ring on Christina's finger bothered Richard. Each second that passed put him closer to his wedding day. He also wondered about the legality of the plan. Logically, it made sense, but laws were never logical. "Yes, but—"

"I don't see how we can fail." Christina placed the bandage in her purse, pulled out her white gloves and put them on. "Not with the two of us working together."

"I agree," Merlin said.

"You came up with the best solution." She kissed Merlin's cheek. "Thank you."

"You would make the most adorable princess bride."

Christina blushed. "You're so sweet."

"And you are a dear." Merlin sighed. "Your Highness, are you certain you do not wish to wed Miss Armstrong?"

"Quite certain." Richard clutched the table. "Are you ready to leave?"

"Yes." Her eyes sparkled. "We've got lots of work to do if we're going to find you a wife in time."

As they walked to the square to meet Didier, Richard took Christina through the residential section of the village. It gave them more cover from the awakening town, and he could afford no more distractions. The sooner they rendezvoused with Didier, the better.

"Do you want to get married in a church or will a civil ceremony do, Your Highness?" Christina asked.

"What?"

"We need to plan your wedding. Once we find you a bride, we won't want to waste a minute."

"I have been looking for a woman to marry for years. Do you really think I am going to find one by the end of the week?"

She raised her gloved hand. "Do you have a choice?"

Did he? Richard hesitated. Christina was the one wearing his ring; she was the one he was supposed to marry. He could do worse. Her firm legs looked even longer in her denim shorts. Shimmering strands of hair peeked out from her hat. The sea air only added to her floral-citrus scent. And her soft lips...

But she was the one chosen by the legend, and the last thing she wanted was to marry a prince. She wanted to marry a cowboy like the one in her sketch. He could not marry her even if he wanted to. "No, I—"

Brakes squealed. A car door slammed. Footsteps sounded. A flash. Yelling.

"There they are!" one voice shouted. "Your Highness!"

"This shot will put my kid through college," another added.

Grabbing Christina's hand, Richard ran up the steep, cobblestoned street. No way would he reward the press with a "shot." He ducked into an alley, stepped inside a doorway and placed Christina between the door and himself.

Click-click. Footsteps sounded. Someone was coming. He put his finger against her soft, full lips to silence her. "On three," he mouthed, "follow me."

She nodded.

The footsteps came closer. "I think they went this way," a man called out.

"Do you think they're out for a lovers' stroll?" another snickered. "Too bad we couldn't catch them at Astarte. I'd like to see Christina's jewels."

The first man chuckled. "So would I, but we'll have to take what we can get."

How about a black eye? The two men infuriated Richard. It was not only them and their disrespect. It was all the press, glorifying the legend, making the citizens of San Montico believe wholeheartedly. His people were totally enchanted—no, obsessed—with magic. He'd had enough.

Richard raised his hand and counted off with his fingers. One. Two. Three.

He burst from the doorway, charging the two men like a stampeding bull. The men tumbled, cursing. Their cameras hit the stone road. It was almost too easy.

But Richard did not look back. One phone call and word would be out—the prince and his fiancée out and about in San Montico. He had to get Christina off the streets before anyone else saw them. An open door beckoned them. Pulling Christina behind him, he slipped inside a courtyard and closed the gate.

Her cheeks flushed, she struggled to catch her breath.

"Are you okay?" Richard asked.

"Yes, but I thought I was in better shape, Your Highness. Those hills are a killer on the thighs."

But what thighs. Time to be a prince, not a man. He looked away.

"Do you think we lost them?"

He listened for footsteps, for any noises on the street. Nothing. "For now."

"Good," she said. "You were impressive back there. Do they teach princes how to do that sort of thing?"

"Yes, we take a class on how to handle the press like true gentlemen."

She chuckled. "I'd love to see how you handle them when you aren't being a gentleman."

If she stayed much longer, she might get the opportunity. "We must hurry if we are to meet Didi."

"But the photographers?"

"We will be...cautious."

Upon their arrival at the village square, Christina watched Prince Richard scan the surrounding roads, then glance at his watch. "Didi knew what time to meet us."

She sat on a concrete bench, removed her baseball cap and brushed her hair with her fingers. She needed a shower and breakfast. "Maybe he got held up at the palace."

"He is always prompt."

"I'm sure he'll be here soon, Your Highness."

He nodded. "At least no one else is here."

Thank goodness. She could use a few minutes to relax after the long walk to the square. Keeping up with Prince Richard's long strides was exhausting but gave her a great view of his cute butt. Not as good as the one she had now with the sheen of sweat covering his arms and his legs and glistening in the sun.

What was she doing?

She shouldn't be gawking at him like a schoolgirl with a crush. She was supposed to help find him a wife. She couldn't afford to be attracted to him. Cute butt or not. "Why don't you sit down, Your Highness?"

Turning, he touched the tip of her nose gently. "It is turning pink. You should put your cap on."

Her skin burned from his touch, not the sun. "I could use a little color."

She stared at his face. His nose was tan, not the slightest bit pink. Her gaze dropped to his lips. They looked sculpted, full and very kissable. Last night's kiss had only whetted her appetite. She wanted another taste.

No, Christina scolded herself. She didn't. She didn't want to kiss him. Not ever again.

"So what are your requirements, Your Highness?"

"Requirements?"

"For a wife."

"I have a list."

She should have known. Prince Richard was too logical for his own good. "Could you give me an idea of what you are looking for?"

"A woman who is educated and from a good family. One who has the ability and desire to bear children. A sense of humor would be helpful. A sense of style is imperative. A love of the water and sailing is important. The ability to speak foreign languages is optional but would be a great asset. And the ability to handle press and publicity is a must."

That counted her out for sure. Not that she wanted to be in the running. "At least I have something to go on."

"I also have the names of the women who did not meet

my requirements on a printout. No sense reinventing the wheel."

A printout? "How many…?"

"Too many."

Just what Christina thought. She, on the other hand, had dated too few. Her painting kept her busy. And even though her parents were always introducing her to potential husband candidates, most of the men were young clones of her father. Absolutely the last type of man she would marry. After a prince, that is. When she moved out west…

Christina focused on the elaborate fountain she saw in the center of the square. Perfectly manicured grass that would be the envy of any country-club groundskeeper surrounded the fountain. As marble dolphins frolicked with a mermaid, water sprayed fifteen feet in the air and cascaded down the three-tiered bowls.

She slipped off her sandals. "Want to cool off?"

"I…"

Not about to give him a chance to say no, she headed to the fountain and climbed in. "This feels so good. Aren't you going to join me?"

Prince Richard looked around. "Why not?"

"That's what I always say."

He pulled off his socks and shoes and climbed in. "This does feel rather refreshing."

The smile on his face reminded her of a little boy's grin. She could imagine Prince Richard as a child with his wavy hair and piercing blue eyes and thousand-watt smile.

"I never would have thought of this myself, Christina."

She splashed him. "Would you have thought of that?"

"Possibly." Grinning, he retaliated, sending a sheet of water her way.

She moved to escape but backed into a dolphin. Trapped. He came closer. And even closer until he stood in front of her. Mere inches away.

His warm breath caressed her neck, sending a surge of desire through her. Water misted down on them but did nothing to cool the heat building inside her.

She read the challenge pooling in his gaze, but she couldn't keep testing the water. A riptide was waiting to drag her out to a raging sea. The logical side of her wanted no part of it. But the other side wanted...

Christina couldn't stare into his eyes without succumbing to his charm. She stepped to one side too quickly and stumbled. His strong arms grabbed her, keeping her upright. He held her for a moment, and she enjoyed the secure feeling of his arms around her. His touch seared her skin through the cotton of her T-shirt. His scent intoxicated her.

He was not a mere mortal. He couldn't be.

"Are you okay?" His eyes shone with concern and something else Christina wasn't sure she wanted to see.

Not trusting her voice, she nodded.

"Be careful. I would not want you to get hurt."

Then stay away from me. Stay far, far away.

Before she could blink, his lips were upon hers. Gentle and tender. So sweet.

And then... The gentleness and tenderness disappeared, replaced by power and hunger and need. Pure, raw, out-of-control passion.

Heaven must taste like Prince Richard because a kiss so all-consuming, so overwhelming, so perfect, could be nothing less than heaven-sent.

Tell me you feel it, too. She touched his chest and felt the pounding of his heart beneath her palm.

His hands splayed across her back, pressing her closer. She leaned into him, returning his fervor with an eagerness of her own. Nothing mattered except this moment, except him. Blood roared through her veins. Sensations pulsed through her. An ache built deep within her. She wanted him; she needed him. "Rich—"

Abruptly, he ended the kiss, and Christina felt a piece of her go with him. "That was…"

He cupped her chin with his hand. "A mistake."

The words echoed in her mind. Disappointment shot straight to her heart. Of course it had been a mistake. So what if his kiss had been earth-shattering? He was too handsome, too charming, too sexy. Too princely. She swallowed hard.

"Christina—"

"It was a mistake, Your Highness." She tilted her chin and met his gaze. "And one we should not repeat."

Chapter Eight

Christina wanted nothing more than to find Richard another woman to marry. Her lips still burned from his kiss, and that only made her angry. Angry at him, angry at herself.

She lugged what felt like a fifty-pound sack of potatoes to her room. Dropping the copies of the *Almanach de Gotha* and other registries of aristocracy, peerage and baronage onto the cherry Queen Anne writing table, she blew out a puff of air.

Damn his kisses; damn him.

She armed herself with a pad of paper and a pen. Sitting at the desk, she listed all the names of women she could think of off the top of her head. Friends, friends of friends, movie stars. She scribbled them down as fast as she could until she had over fifty names. She read over the list. A good start, but most of these women were Americans. Richard might prefer a bride with royal bloodlines in her family, given what had happened with Thea.

Oh, well. Christina patted the stack of thick books.

That's what the peerage registries were for. Thank goodness the palace library had copies.

Opening one of the tomes, she scanned the first entry, the second, the third. Such small print. She squinted and blinked and continued to the fourth. An unwelcome image of Richard filled her mind.

At the fountain, he had made her feel sexy and vibrantly alive. A way she'd never felt before. Surely he had felt something during the kiss even if it had been a mistake. His heart *had* been pounding as rapidly as hers.

What was she thinking? She shouldn't care what he felt. It had been just a kiss. A kiss that hadn't changed anything. Richard had plans of his own; so did she. Okay, maybe not plans, but she did hope to move out west where she'd be more likely to find the man of her dreams. Marrying a prince was not part of the picture, and becoming a princess was out of the question.

She returned to the book. Here was one: ABERCON-WAY, Sir Anthony Robert Henry, Baronet. His daughter, Elizabeth Mary, had been born in March of 1974. That would make her old enough. As of this printing, she was listed as unattached. That would make her single. Christina wrote Elizabeth Aberconway's name on the list marked Royalty.

This would be easier than Christina realized, especially if she searched by date of birth. She set to work. Soon she had five more names on the list.

The telephone rang. She answered the phone sitting on the desk. "Hello?"

"Hello, darling."

Though Christina wasn't used to the endearment, she recognized the voice. "Mother."

"Thank goodness I reached you before I left. Have your feet touched the ground yet? I know mine haven't. I'm exhausted. I need to take care of a few last-minute details before I leave for New York." Claire finally took a breath. "Talk about a busy morning."

Morning for Claire Armstrong began at noon. Or usually did. Christina did a quick time conversion and realized it was very early for her mother to be up and about. "Are you okay, Mother?"

"I'm perfectly splendid," she answered in a cheery voice. "Once I arrive in New York, I'm heading over to Bergdorf's. We must look our best for the royal family."

As well as talking on the phone, Claire had shopping down to an art form. "There's no need to go to so much trouble."

"It's no trouble. I did have a hand in this. If it weren't for me, you would never have attended the prince's birthday ball. Didn't I say going to San Montico was the right thing to do?"

"You did."

"Oh, darling, you must be so delighted."

"'Delighted' doesn't begin to describe how I feel." Christina sighed.

"I can tell, my sweet. How are the wedding plans coming along?"

"Daddy and Princess Marguerite seem to have everything under control."

"The princess's charity galas are always *très magnifique*. She has exquisite taste."

Everything about her was exquisite. Richard's wife would need to have the same quality or she might feel overshadowed. Someone mousy wouldn't do. "She does."

"Kelsey will be arriving shortly. She'll be able to offer some assistance. She's the wedding planner extraordinaire."

Kelsey. Can't forget her. Christina jotted her cousin's name on the non-royalty list, then drew a line through it. Kelsey had been dragged through her parents' bitter divorce and swore she would never marry even though she loved coordinating other people's weddings.

"And you, my baby, will be the princess extraordinaire."

Pride oozed from each of Claire's words and made Christina squirm in her seat. Her mother would have a nervous breakdown when Richard married someone else. "I'm not a princess yet."

"Simply a technicality. You will be royalty," Claire gushed. "I could almost cry. I have cried."

Any more of this and Christina was going to cry. Once again she would disappoint her parents. Once again it would be very public. She'd finally gotten the attention she'd longed for from them, but Christina couldn't marry just to please her parents. No matter how much she might want their love. "Mother—"

"I knew something like this would happen to you one day. Your grandfather always said you were a slow starter. If only he could be here, too. Remember how he used to call you Princess?"

"I remember." All this attention for something that wasn't going to happen. Christina felt lower than pond scum.

"My friends are so jealous. Why, Serena Worthington is simply beside herself. She can't understand why Laurel wasn't invited to the ball, and I hated to state the obvious."

Christina scanned her list, ready to make a notation. "What's wrong with Laurel?"

"She's pregnant," Claire whispered. "And starting to show. That's not the worst of it, either. They're also facing financial ruin and scandal. I wouldn't think either Serena or Laurel could face anyone right now."

So much for her. Christina scratched Laurel Worthington's name from the list.

"I faxed your father a few names to add to the guest list.

I know it's short notice, but no one would dare turn down a royal wedding invite. It'll be the social event of the season.

"Oh, and I called Mitzy Hollis-Montgomery. Well, she told me the worst news. Her daughter, Thea, is miserable being married to King Gustav of Heidel. She wants a divorce, but divorce is illegal in his country. Can you imagine? Of course, she deserves everything she gets. She always did strike me as a gold digger of the worst kind."

Christina hated gossip. "That's a terrible thing to say, Mother."

"Yes, but her loss was our gain."

Was it? If Richard found out about Thea's unhappy marriage. It wouldn't change a thing, Christina realized, feeling more relieved than she should.

She studied the names on her list. Some of the women she'd met at parties or weddings or charity dinners. Others she knew by name only. The woman Richard married had to be good enough not only for him, but also for San Montico. She had to meet certain criteria.

Claire knew everything about everyone who was anyone. She would know the intimate details and be able to help weed out the undeserving. Christina hated to use her mother for information, but her options were limited. She readied her pen. "So, Mom, do you have time to go over the guest list with me? I don't want to leave anyone out."

Two hours passed. By the time Claire finished going through the guest list and then some, Christina had received useful information and eliminated more than forty names—women who were now engaged or married or having affairs or having babies or in the midst of some emotional crisis.

"Well, darling, it's been a pleasure chatting with you, but I must run. I need to finish packing. I can't wait to see the palace or meet your prince.

"I'm taking the Concorde to Paris to pick up a few more

things. I've been doing a little shopping for your trousseau.''

"I don't need a trousseau."

"Of course you do. You must have clothes suitable for a princess.''

"But—"

"Don't worry, I'll buy only the best. Call if you need anything, darling. Otherwise I'll speak with you when I arrive on Wednesday. Plenty of time to assist with the final wedding arrangements and help you pack for the honeymoon.''

It was all Christina could do to say bye and hang up.

Her honeymoon.

It was something she couldn't contemplate; something that would never happen. Yet she couldn't help herself. The image of her and Richard spending the days getting to know one another, spending the nights making love, made Christina want to rip her list of wife candidates to shreds, light a match to the pieces and toss the ashes out the window.

Those thoughts, those feelings, made zero sense. Okay, she was a sucker for romance, but this was too much.

Christina removed her left glove. The diamond glimmered in the natural light. She tugged on the ring, pulling again and again. The gold band still wouldn't budge.

She held her hand out in front of her and addressed the ring. "Don't you see? Richard is not the man for me, and I'm not the woman for him. If you are an enchanted ring, please use your magic and come off.''

She tried to remove it again.

Nothing.

So much for magic.

Could it be magic?

Christina could only wonder.

A beautiful blue cocktail dress, designed by Delia, arrived at her room along with an invitation to a party to celebrate the upcoming royal nuptials. She didn't want to wear it, but a maid came to help her dress and Christina couldn't say no.

Standing in the ballroom, she was happy she'd worn the dress. The fabric shimmered beneath the lights and flowed around her with every movement. She wanted to twirl around until she was dizzy enough to pass out.

Not that she wasn't dizzy already—thanks to Princess Marguerite's intimate soiree with one hundred of her closest friends. As enchanting and lovely as Christina could have imagined, the palace came alive with the wonder of the legend. Whimsical decorations, a string quartet and scrumptious food set the fairy-tale mood. Once again she felt like Cinderella at the ball.

Floating from group to group, she reveled in the congratulations of the well-wishers. To her right, Princess Marguerite smiled and laughed with a baron and baroness. Christina had never seen her look so happy, so alive. The princess looked positively glowing in her sparkling celadon gown. To her left, the marquess flirted with women half his age, enjoying every minute of it. In front of Christina, her father was in his element, schmoozing and networking with the European elite. So much happiness.

And then she saw Richard. He was chatting to the guests as was required of him, but Christina could tell by the strained smile, minus the dimple, on his face and the distant look in his eyes that he was just tolerating the party.

As she should be.

But...

Listening to the sincere words of joy as the guests celebrated and toasted her upcoming marriage, seeing the genuine delight on their faces and feeling their complete acceptance of her in the inner circle of royals made her feel like a princess bride-to-be.

Believe it or not, she liked the feeling.

But she couldn't allow such thoughts. In the heel of her shoe, she carried her list of wife candidates for Richard. Every time she took a step, the paper pressed against her heel, giving her a constant reminder.

The wonderful words the guests said about her and the wedding weren't true. Nor would they come true. All of this was a sham, a lie. Thinking in those terms made Christina want to run and hide.

Instead, she escaped the festivities through a pair of French doors and sought refuge on the terrace. Tonight had nothing to do with her, she realized, but everything to do with the ring.

The ring.

Her finger felt bare, and she glanced at her hand. The outline beneath her glove told her the ring was still there, but for a moment, she had forgotten it was on her finger. Regret mingled with relief. Part of her wanted the ring to be gone, to have disappeared or fallen off somewhere, never to be found again. But the other part wanted...

What was she going to do?

Christina clutched the stone rail and took a deep breath. The cool night air carried the faint scents of gardenias, roses and salt. The moon illuminated the sky full of twinkling white stars. Insects composed a symphony complete with a cicada percussion section, and a breeze rustled through the large leafy trees, tying the island sounds together.

"I thought you might be out here, sweetheart."

Turning, Christina saw her father walk toward her. The grinning father of the bride carried two flutes of champagne. She'd never seen him look so happy. Her heart ached as she realized how disappointed he would be with her when Richard married someone else. "I needed some fresh air."

"It's been a long evening. Some of the guests are starting to leave." He handed her one of the glasses. "Quite a party, wouldn't you say?"

"It's been...interesting." So many dukes, duchesses, counts and countesses. After reading all those names in the peerage registries, she never expected to meet so many of them tonight. "But I wish—"

"Tell me what you want, and I'll get it for you."

Now that she was going to marry a prince, everything had changed. Whatever she wanted. No more lectures. No more disappointing looks. No more wanting what she couldn't have. Too bad it couldn't last. "I just wish...this was all over."

Alan smiled. "It'll be over soon."

Not soon enough. She took a sip of her champagne.

"I'm having my lawyers draw up the necessary papers."

Her father would never understand that the kind of man she wanted to marry could not care less about her family's fortune. And in this case... "A prenup is not necessary."

"Prince Richard seems honorable enough, but it's for your own protection."

"I've never wanted any of your—"

"Let me take care of business. I've been around long enough to know what precautions to take."

"You're not old, Daddy."

"Perhaps not in age, but around you..." He smoothed her hair, the same way he used to do when she was a little girl. She resisted the urge to throw herself into her father's arms and ask him to make things right. "One minute we were bringing you home from the hospital and the next you're getting married. Where did the years go?"

Board meetings, business trips, vacations, work...

She finished off her champagne. "Time flies when you're having fun."

"Is something wrong, Christina?"

"Things are happening so fast, Daddy. Too fast. I mean, we just met the de Thierrys and suddenly we're all chummy and Mom's buying my trousseau and Delia's making me a wedding gown..." The words poured from Christina's mouth faster than jumbo shrimp disappeared from a buffet, but she couldn't help herself. She had to say them, get them out. "Don't you think we should take a break? Slow down? Postpone things a while?"

"If you don't marry Prince Richard, he'll lose his throne. You don't want that to happen, do you?"

She glanced at the gardens below. "No."

"I didn't think so." He lifted her chin with his fingertip. "I know you've been rather sheltered and haven't had much...experience with men, but—"

"I'm not worried about that."

The aha expression in his eyes brought a sigh to his lips. "Good, because that's your mother's department."

Christina nodded.

"Your mother was a nervous wreck before our wedding. She was certain everything would go wrong, but nothing did."

"She always told me it was the happiest day of her life."

"And yours will be just as happy." He gave her shoulder a reassuring squeeze. "I've taken care of everything. Your wedding will be perfect."

"It's not the wedding. It's—"

The sound of footsteps made her pause. She saw Richard walking on the terrace toward them, his brow furrowed. "Is there a problem?"

Alan laughed. "A case of prewedding jitters, that's all."

Richard stared at her. "Are you okay, Christina?"

"I'm fine, Your Highness." She said the words with only the slightest hesitation.

"That's my girl." Alan raised his glass to her. "Your mother and I are so proud of you. We always knew you would make something of yourself one day and not whittle away your life drawing your little pictures."

Christina tried to ignore her father's words and the way they pricked her soul. No one in her family understood her. She didn't fit the image of a successful Armstrong. In a family full of doctors, lawyers, politicians, scientists and business executives, an artist just didn't belong. Christina was only one of two Armstrongs who hadn't gone to graduate school, but even her cousin Kelsey had found success as the wedding consultant to the stars.

"I think it is wonderful that Christina paints portraits of pets," Richard said. "Not everyone has such a gift. In fact, I would like to commission a portrait of my horse, Beauté du Diable. That is, if you would do me the honor."

Honor? He was only being polite. Still...

Christina's heart beat faster; her chest tightened. She couldn't breathe; she felt warm. She blinked back the tears stinging the corners of her eyes. In that moment, she wanted to throw her arms around Richard and hug him and kiss him and marry him. Okay, maybe not marry him, but everything else. "I'd be delighted to paint Beauté du Diable."

Devil's Beauty. What an interesting name for Richard's horse.

Alan smiled. "She's a wonderful painter, Your Highness."

No matter how much her clients praised her work, she had always hoped her parents would see the positive side of what she did. Maybe times were changing.

"And the portrait would make a wonderful wedding present," he added.

So much for the praise. Her father was only trying to please the prince. Christina stared at the moon.

"We must thank my mother for the party." Richard took her arm. "Please excuse us."

"Certainly, Your Highness." Her father moved out of the way.

Richard led her back inside. The party was still going strong. All eyes seemed to be upon them, watching their every move. Christina hated the feeling. The last thing she'd ever wanted was to be the center of attention.

"People are staring," she whispered.

"Ignore them," he ordered as if it were the easiest thing in the world to pretend no one was watching them. "As soon as we speak with my mother, we will make our getaway."

"We can't leave." Christina, of all people, should be the last one to remind him of etiquette. "The party's in our honor."

"I can do what I want." He winked. "I am the prince."

"Do you know what people will think if we waltz out of here together?"

"Fine." He held out his hand. "We'll tango."

"Your Highness." She tried not to smile as she took his hand.

"People will think exactly what we want them to think." As he stared deep into her eyes and made her feel like the only other person in the palace, her heart beat in double time.

Christina stood mesmerized. Tingles ran down the length of her and back up again as if someone had sprinkled fairy dust all over her. "And what might that be?"

"That we are falling in love and excited to marry."

Funny, but when he looked at her like that, she almost believed it herself.

Richard could not believe it. Every time he had looked at his mother, he did a double take. Of all the times for her to stop wearing black and have a French manicure. Yes, he wanted her to stop mourning, but not because of the Legend of the Ring.

The Legend.

Who needed an enchanted ring to find a bride? Not when he had his mother, who was relishing the role of match-maker. Marguerite had been more than understanding about their leaving the party. She had even suggested a walk through the gardens and practically pushed them out the door with an order to find the moonlight. Anything to bring him and Christina together; anything for grandchildren.

And much to his dismay, it was working.

He could not allow that to happen. He had already been thinking about Christina too much. He didn't believe in magic, but this in-his-face matchmaking was hard to ignore. Richard could not give in. He needed to avoid anything that would be considered or construed as romantic. Instead of a walk, he brought Christina to his office, the safest, least romantic place in all the palace. Or so he thought. Now he wasn't so certain.

She sighed. "I don't know how you get any work done with a view like this."

He turned his gaze from the dots of light from the village, flickering below and decorating the hillside like tiny stars, to Christina. She wore her hair in a single French braid that accentuated the graceful curve of her neck. Her pale blue cocktail dress fell midthigh, showing a tantalizing amount of skin. Quite an enchanting view. "I do what I must."

"I'm sure you do." She faced him. "How was your afternoon?"

The Arts Council wanted his approval on their new budget and two-hundred-page mission statement. The

Royal Council could not agree on anything, and a vital trade agreement was at an impasse. A typical day for him. "Fine. I had the usual amount of work waiting for me."

"I got some work done, too." She removed her right shoe and pulled out a folded piece of paper from her heel.

As she tried to put on her shoe, she teetered and clutched the chair behind his desk. The shoe fell to the floor.

"Allow me." Richard knelt on one knee and picked up her shoe. As he placed the shoe on her foot, he wanted to caress the arch of her foot, linger around her slim ankle. He forced himself to rise. "What were you carrying in your shoe?"

Christina unfolded the paper. "Before I show you this, I want to say thank-you. Not only for helping with my shoe, but for what you said to my father about my paintings." She smoothed out the creases. "It was…nice and meant a lot to me."

Richard smiled. "I do want you to paint Beauté du Diable."

"Really? But you've never seen one of my portraits."

"I saw your sketch of the cowboy and his horse."

"The cowboy?"

"In your room this morning."

"Oh, right." She smoothed the folds from the paper. "But a sketch is different from a portrait. For all you know, I could be color-blind or a terrible painter."

"The way your eyes dance and your smile lights up your face when you talk about your work tells me you are none of those things. You love what you do so much, you must be talented." Her shy smile stirred something deep within him. "No one, not even your family, should belittle what you do."

"My family has—how should I put this?—high expectations." She placed the paper on his desk and ran her fingertips along the edge of his leather chair. "Do you know what I used to...? Never mind."

He leaned toward her, curious about her wistful tone. "Tell me."

"It's silly."

He sat on the edge his desk. "We have all done silly things in our lives."

She raised an eyebrow. "Even you?"

"Perhaps once or twice."

Christina laughed. "That many?"

He shrugged. "If I tell you something silly, will you tell me yours?"

"Okay."

He wasn't accustomed to opening up and letting anyone in, but something about Christina... "When I was seven, my father bought me a baseball glove and took me to a Yankees game. I still remember the smell of the newly cut grass and how the hot dog tasted. I had never eaten a hot dog before. I caught a foul ball. It was the most perfect day of my life."

"Sounds almost magical."

"It was." He still had the foul ball somewhere. The glove, too. Funny, but he hadn't thought about his trip to Yankee Stadium in years. Not until now. Not until Christina came into his life. "I used to dream of being a major league baseball player. I wanted to be voted to the All-Star game, win a Gold Glove and be selected MVP of the World Series." He smiled at the memory. "See? Silly."

She smiled, too. "I don't think it's silly at all."

"It was when my life was determined before I was even born." Richard sighed. "Your turn."

Almost shyly, Christina glanced up at him. The tip of her tongue darted out and she licked her lower lip. "When I was younger, I used to think I'd been switched at birth. That somewhere out there was a girl, a true Armstrong, who didn't fit in where she was, and if we could trade places, everything would be fine. She could snack on caviar. I could eat Cheez Whiz.''

"Cheez Whiz?"

"It's so good, but my mother would die if she knew I liked it better than caviar.'' Christina smiled. "I told you it's silly, but I'd daydream about what her parents, my real parents had we not been switched, would be like.''

"Tell me about them."

"Well, her dad worked at a gas station. He would leave early so he could watch her perform in a school play or attend one of her art shows. He always had an encouraging word to say and a hug to give. Her mom was always home and loved to cook, especially cookies and cakes. She also sewed and didn't care what colors or hemlines were in for the season.''

"Did you ever tell your parents?"

"Are you kidding? They'd have gotten me involved in some charity to show me how good I had it.'' She hesitated. "I know I have it better than most, but is it so bad to want…?''

"What?"

"Less, no…more. Not clothes or jewelry or a fancy car or a big house. But more family, more time, more…love.''

Until that moment, Richard never knew how good he'd had it, how much he had taken for granted. His entire life he had been surrounded by people who accepted him, supported him, loved him. His family had always been there for him; they would always be there for him come what may. Whereas Christina…

He swallowed hard. Cupping her chin with his hand, he lifted her face to his. Golden freckles dotted the bridge of her nose; a rosy glow colored her cheeks. "There is nothing wrong with wanting more. Everyone I know wants more.''

"Do you?'' She blinked, her lashes fluttering like a pair

of butterfly wings. Her lips parted slightly. Pink and full and soft. Lips meant for wide smiles; lips meant for slow, wet kisses.

Yes, he wanted more.

He wanted her.

Desire hit him like a line drive to third base. He lowered his mouth to hers and touched her lips gently. Warm and inviting.

"Richard," she whispered, and a shudder ran through him.

Not Your Highness.

But Richard.

He pulled her close, probed deeper, exploring and tasting. Her kiss was ambrosia. He wanted more, so much more. Hunger and need took over. His mouth pressed harder with an urgency that surprised, almost embarrassed him. She moaned, and the sound nearly pushed him over the edge. He pulled her even closer; the hard length of him pressed against her.

Unprepared for such a traitorous response from his own flesh, Richard pulled back, but Christina followed him— her lips never leaving his. The most divine method of sweet torture. Over the material of her dress, he cupped her breast. She arched her back and whispered his name.

Again.

Damn, how he wanted her; he wanted to make love with her.

But he could not.

This woman held the key to his future—the key to his throne. Panic battled with desire. Fighting to retain control, Richard tore himself away. He stared at Christina, her eyes wide and confused, her lips red and swollen. He could not do this to either of them. His heart would never belong to her, and hers was waiting to fall in love with a cowboy.

"Christina—"

"Don't worry, I know this doesn't change anything." She tucked a stray piece of hair back into her braid. "It must be the full moon."

Or something else.

"You are going to make some woman very, very happy, Your Highness."

"Thank you," he said, genuinely touched by the compliment.

She picked up the piece of paper she'd taken from her shoe and held it out to him. "We'd better get to work so we can find her."

Chapter Nine

The situation was getting more difficult and complicated by the hour, and Richard was back in his office and unsure what to do. Last night, he had researched the names on Christina's list while she continued searching the registries. All that hard work for what?

Surely not a photograph of them kissing in the fountain.

Seeing the kiss in print jolted Richard from his years of studied indifference. Before meeting Christina, it had not mattered, but now... He could still feel the residue of her kiss. The softness of her lips, the candy-sweet taste of her mouth.

What angered him most was that the picture showed more than a kiss; it showed his raw desire for Christina. Something he had pretended not to feel yesterday. Something he had ignored last night. Something clear for the world to see today.

He had been so captivated by Christina the sky could have been filled with a swarm of locusts and he would not have noticed. Not even Thea had made him feel so...

A definite setback toward proving the legend false, but it was more than that.

Another glimpse at the front page of the morning newspaper, and Richard shook with rage. No one had the right to invade his privacy like that. He slammed the newspaper on his desk, front page down. "How dare they?"

Sitting on the other side of his desk, Didier stirred his steaming cup of Earl Grey. "This isn't the first time you've been photographed kissing a woman, Your Highness."

But it was not the same. Richard rubbed his tired eyes. "Who took the photo?"

"I do not know, Your Highness." Didier added a lump of sugar to his cup. "The picture is on the cover of both the *Times* and the *Journal*. Perhaps if you grant an interview or two after your visit to the Children's Hospital?"

Richard remembered the press coverage of his courtship, engagement and breakup with Thea. It had compounded an already nightmarish situation and turned his subsequent pursuit of a bride into a joke. He only hoped they would not hound Christina after their "breakup." The last thing he wanted was for her to suffer the way he had. "No interviews."

"A statement might ease some of the...tension with the media."

"I will give them a statement when I am ready to give one."

Didier sipped his tea, then placed the cup on a saucer sitting on the edge of the desk. "Without any interviews or statements, they are forced to create their own stories or go to extreme measures to find the truth, Your Highness."

Richard pointed to the newspaper. "That is not the truth."

"You *are* kissing her," Didier pointed out. "It doesn't appear as if anyone is forcing you, Your Highness."

Richard did not appreciate Didier's smile. "It was a mistake."

And the kiss last night? Would that end up in this evening's edition?

Christina's kisses made him feel as though he had found Shangri-la. What was wrong with him? A few kisses, however wonderful, meant nothing.

Didier flipped over the newspaper and stole a glance at the photograph. "That is the kind of mistake I'd like to make."

"You do not understand. When Christina sees the picture... She hates the press for this very reason."

"So you are not angry at the picture, but upset because it will hurt Christina?"

"I am angry about both."

Didier grinned.

"Why are you smiling?"

"You are beginning to care for her, Your Highness."

"No, I am not." Richard did not care for Christina. Not in the way Didi thought. Not in *that* way.

Richard respected her; he liked her. Her intelligence, her sense of humor, her warmth. They made a fine team.

A team—not a couple.

"She is...nice." Richard ignored Didier's raised brow. "She is also the only other person who does not believe in the legend."

"She will make a wonderful wife and a fine princess."

"Yes. No." Didier's hopeful tone was too contagious, but Richard could not allow himself to be caught up in the wedding fever. "She will be a good wife...for someone else. Not for me."

He might be obsessed by her and her kisses. She might haunt his thoughts and his dreams. His feelings, however, had nothing to do with love and marriage, but everything to do with lust and attraction.

Any man would be attracted to Christina Armstrong.

But he would not fall in love and marry her. She was not the woman for him. She was the one chosen by the legend. He wanted nothing to do with her, but his throne was on the line. Once the ring was off her finger...

"Are you willing to abdicate, Your Highness?"

Richard stared out the window. The sun was rising on his island. Golden rays filtered down from the sky, glimmering on patches of dew on the grass-covered hillsides like newly polished silver.

Every morning the scene was the same. The village woke from a peaceful night's rest and slowly came to life. Tendrils of smoke rose from the seventeenth-century chimneys. In the streets, vendors set up stands to sell their food and wares. Carriages delivered milk and eggs to the cottages. Fishing boats from the marina set sail in the calm sea.

"Trust me, Didi. It will not come to that."

Richard loved San Montico with all his heart, but he would not allow himself to become a part of an archaic legend's legacy. He would not allow San Montico to be stuck in the past. He would not allow his heart to be broken again. "I will keep my throne."

"So you will marry, Your Highness?"

Richard hesitated. "I will marry."

Just not Christina.

Ordronneau, Orsak, Orsini, Osorno, Ostenburg, Ostrander.

The letters blurred and Christina rubbed her eyes. Somewhere, hidden among the hundreds of pages and minuscule typeface of this book, was Richard's future wife.

It was up to Christina to find her. She couldn't let his rock-her-world kisses stop her from doing what needed to be done. If only her thoughts would stop straying...

She glanced at her sketchbook. The only thing getting

done this morning was her drawing, but somehow the rider wasn't the cowboy she'd first imagined. The story of Patricia and her prince on a stallion must be the new inspiration. That was the only logical explanation. Christina closed the pad and forced her attention back on the peerage registry.

A knock sounded at her door. "Come in."

Richard stepped into the room, carrying a newspaper. "Good morning."

She smoothed her hair and smiled. "Hi."

"Have you found...anything?"

The piece of paper on the desk was nearly blank except for a few doodles. She was beginning to be as picky as Richard when it came to finding a qualified princess and had found only four names. "A few possibilities."

"Good," he said. "Did you receive your schedule for today?"

She nodded. "Appearance at Children's Hospital at ten, lunch at noon, and a jam-packed afternoon. I'm sure yours is worse."

"It is." He unfolded the newspaper and held it out to her. "I have something to show you."

Christina stared at the photograph on the front page of the *San Montico Times*. No. This couldn't be happening. Her stomach knotted; her breath caught in her throat.

The photograph made her look so wanton, so needy. It was right there in black and white for the world to see. Her emotions and attraction to Richard crystal clear. "I thought we were alone."

"So did I."

She looked away, trying to focus her gaze on the open page of the registry. "I'm so sorry."

He raised her chin with his fingertips and gazed into her eyes. "You did nothing wrong, Christina. Nothing."

"But...everyone will see it. They will think—"

"Yes, they will, and for that *I* am sorry. I should have known better." Richard stroked her face with his thumb. "What happened at the fountain was private, not meant to be displayed on the front page of newspapers."

The tenderness of his touch made her want to hold on to him and never let go. But Christina couldn't allow herself to think that way. She shouldn't want his arms around her. She shouldn't crave his closeness. She shouldn't feel anything for him. "I only wish we hadn't..."

"Do not let this worry you." He rolled up the paper and dropped it into the wastebasket next to the desk. "This type of publicity is to be expected, and it is too late to do anything about it."

She knew he was right. "But it's still horrible. How do you stand it?"

Richard shrugged. "One learns to tolerate it."

"I don't think I ever will." She couldn't wait until she lived out in the middle of nowhere, where no one knew who she was, where no one cared if she was an Armstrong or not. "It's like living in a fishbowl and having the entire world watching your every move."

"You will not have to put up with it for much longer."

She fingered the ring with her right hand, feeling a combination of relief and sadness. "I know."

The trip to the Children's hospital helped Christina put things into perspective. The photograph on the front page of the paper no longer seemed important. Not when so many children were suffering from illnesses or injuries.

Despite the antiseptic smell and sterile surroundings, Christina was enjoying herself. To see the doctors, nurses and administrators falling over themselves to speak with Richard was humorous in itself. But it was the children who made her day.

The excitement at meeting the prince had their eyes sparkling and their mouths smiling. The difference Richard made with a bedside visit amazed her. He might have said only a few words, but that was enough. He carried himself proudly and with confidence and was a prince the children could respect and love. When they gave him crayon drawn pictures, he praised the drawings, making the children feel as if they had given him priceless Monets.

As Richard spoke with a small group of nurses, Christina strolled down the hall. A door, slightly ajar, caught her attention. She hadn't remembered visiting the room and peeked inside. A uniformed nurse was standing by a lone bed that sat near a window. A little girl, around six or seven, with white bandages covering her eyes, lay in the bed sniffling, her shoulders shaking.

"I want to draw the prince a picture." The little girl sobbed. "All the other children got to."

The nurse patted her shoulder. "I'm sorry, but I don't have time to help you, Sonia. I'm sure he'll understand."

"No, he'll be mad at me," the little girl insisted. "Please give me my crayons. I want to try."

Christina watched the scene with a sense of déjà vu. She remembered how she would want to do some project or craft when she was younger but could find no one to help her. Her parents would be away, the housekeeping staff would be busy, and her nanny would not want to clean up the mess. Luckily, things changed once her grandfather moved in.

Every child, whether in the hospital or not, deserved to have someone give them a little help, love and attention when they needed it most.

Pushing the door open, she stuck her head inside the room and saw Sonia's lips quiver. It was all Christina could do not to rush over to the bed and hold the little girl close as she had wished someone would have done with her. "Excuse me?"

The nurse turned when Christina entered. "Aren't you—"

She raised her gloved hand to stop the nurse from saying any more. "If it's okay, I can help her draw a picture."

"That's very kind of you." The nurse handed her some coloring paper and a box of crayons. "She's recovering from an operation and has been restless today."

As the nurse left the room, Christina walked to the bed. "Hello, Sonia. My name's Christina."

Sonia's mouth formed a small O. "Are you the one who's going to marry the prince?"

"I'm the one who's wearing the ring," she admitted.

"Are you really going to help me draw a picture for the prince?"

"Yes, I am."

Sonia straightened and placed her hands on the bed tray. "Can you draw?"

"I've had a little experience."

Sonia knocked over a plastic cup. Water trickled onto the bed tray and her lips quivered again. "I'm sorry."

"Don't worry about it." Christina set the art supplies on the bed, grabbed a tissue and blotted the water. "This is nothing compared with some of the things I've spilled."

Sonia's frown disappeared and she laughed. "And you can even see."

"My 20/20 vision hasn't kept me from spilling, though I wish it had. I'm sure my parents do, too." Christina opened the box of crayons. "What would you like to draw?"

"Flowers. And birds, too."

This would be easy. She placed the sheet of paper on the bed tray. "Where should we start?"

"The sun." Sonia tilted her head. "But I haven't seen it in so long."

"Let's try to refresh your memory." Christina hesitated

until she saw a medical device with a bulb. She turned it on and held it near Sonia's hands. "Tell me what this feels like."

"It feels warm." Sonia drew her hands away. "Hot."

"That's what the sun looks like...hot." Christina flicked off the light. "Do you remember your colors?"

"I think so."

"What color does hot feel like?"

"Red." Sonia giggled. "Red hot."

"Red it is." Christina handed Sonia the crayon and placed her hand in the center of the paper. "Go ahead."

Sonia hesitated. "What do I draw?"

Christina brushed her fingers through Sonia's soft hair. "Draw what hot feels like."

Smiling, Sonia went to work and colored a wild patch of red in the center of the white paper. As Christina watched, she thought about having children of her own. She would make sure her children had all the love and attention they needed. No nanny or housekeeper would sit up with them at night if they got sick. If Christina took a vacation, her children would come along. And she wouldn't care whether they wanted to be a scientist or a store clerk so long as they were happy.

"That's a glorious sun."

"Can I add some clouds?"

"Sure." Christina grabbed a cotton ball from a nearby counter and placed it in Sonia's small hand. "Here's a cloud."

Sonia giggled. "You can't touch clouds."

"Well, today you can."

The little girl squeezed the white puff and touched it to her face. "It's soft and fluffy." Sonia wrinkled her nose. "What color are clouds?"

Christina's heart caught in her throat. "What color would you like them to be?"

"Purple." Sonia's smile widened. "Purple clouds sound nice."

"Yes, they do." Christina handed her the purple crayon. "Here you go."

Sonia was so precious. As she colored purple clouds, some round, others mere lines, Christina wiped a tear from her eye. She hoped Sonia's operation would help her regain her sight. If it didn't, maybe Christina's parents could help. They might not be good at providing unconditional love, but when it came to charitable donations, they were generous to a fault.

"We need the birds now," Sonia announced. "And the flowers, too."

Birds? Flowers? Christina couldn't see anything resembling a feather or a petal.

Excited, Sonia fidgeted in her bed. "May we draw blue birds and yellow birds and green birds and black birds? And some roses and daisies?"

"Yes, but it looks like we're going to have to wing it."

Sonia's shoulders sagged. "We don't have to finish the picture."

"Oh, yes, we do." Christina grabbed a green crayon and took Sonia's hand in hers. "But it's going to be a joint effort."

Thank goodness he had escaped the gaggle of nurses. Richard appreciated all they did for the children, but enough was enough. Hearing his family talk about the wedding was one thing, but to hear the nurses, his subjects... One mention of the word "wedding," and the cackling had begun. He was realizing how fortunate he was that Christina wore the ring. Any other woman would be busy planning the wedding, not trying to find him another bride.

Richard walked down the hospital hall. Christina had to be around here somewhere. He passed an open door and saw her back as she stood at the bedside of a patient. He could not tell what they were doing, but he could hear giggles. Sounding as beautiful as the bells of the cathedral, the laughter of Christina and a child touched his heart.

It did not surprise him to find her there. She had made each child feel so cherished and important. She would be a wonderful mother when she had children of her own.

He imagined Christina wearing the de Thierry tiara and dancing with him. He pictured her holding his hand and waving to their subjects as they rode through the streets in the royal carriage. He envisioned her holding their baby and presenting the new heir to all of San Montico.

It was becoming much too easy to imagine a future with her. Something too risky, too dangerous to even consider. The last time he felt this way was with Thea, and like his ex-fiancée, Christina did not love him. He needed to stop thinking about her and find another woman to marry.

"One of the nurses said he was the most handsome man in the world," a high-pitched voice said. "Is he?"

"Just between you and me, yes, he is," Christina answered in a confidential whisper.

"What does he look like?"

Richard stepped inside the room and saw the bandages on the little girl's eyes. He should let them know he was here. He started to but could not. He wanted to hear Christina's answer.

She held the little girl's hand and leaned close. "He looks...like the most handsome prince from your dreams or your favorite fairy tale. His eyes are as clear and blue as a mountain stream. His smile could charm a mouse out of its last crumb of cheese. He's tall and strong and everything a prince should be."

Was that how Christina saw him? Richard froze. His heart started beating in double time.

The little girl sat up. "Who's there?"

Turning, Christina's eyes widened. She stared at him for a moment, then motioned him over.

"Who is it?" the little girl asked. "The nurse?"

"It's the prince," Christina whispered. "Your Highness, may I present one of your most loyal subjects, Miss Sonia."

Richard stepped forward, tearing his gaze from his fianc—Christina. "I am delighted to make your acquaintance, Miss Sonia." He placed a kiss on the back of her tiny hand. Sonia released a small sigh. Giggling, she pulled her hand away and covered her mouth. "How are you feeling today?"

"Fine, Your Highness."

He saw the crayons and a mass of color on a piece of paper. "I see you've drawn a picture."

Sonia patted the bed tray for her drawing and held it up. "It's for you, Your Highness."

Richard stared at the drawing. He wasn't sure what to make of the picture, but it was colorful. "It's beautiful."

"Do you know what it is, Your Highness?" Sonia asked.

The picture resembled abstract art. Richard studied the drawing closer. Christina tapped him on the shoulder, pointed out the window and flapped her arms. "I see birds flying in the sky."

"Christina helped me draw those."

"Did she? They're very…birdlike." He looked at Christina, who merely smiled. Richard had no doubt she had used her artistic talent to help with the drawing and her natural friendliness to encourage the little girl. "The red must be the sun."

Sonia nodded happily. "It is, Your Highness. It is."

"And the purple…" At a loss, he glanced at Christina, who mouthed the necessary word. "Must be clouds."

"Yes. Do you see the yellow flowers?"

"Oh, yes. I see a field of flowers."

Sonia tilted her chin. "I—I hope you like it, Your Highness."

"I love it, Sonia. Thank you." Richard held her small hand. "And I know the perfect place to display it."

"Really, Your Highness?"

"Yes, really."

And he meant it. Sonia and all the children had been delightful. He wanted to do something for them. A display of their drawings in the Public Hall would be a start. He smiled. Christina was rubbing off on him. In more ways than one. He drew in a breath, and his mouth went dry.

Sonia yawned.

"Your Highness," Christina said, "Sonia worked hard on your drawing. Perhaps we should allow her to rest."

"Of course." As Christina headed toward the door, Sonia sank onto her pillow. Richard covered her with a blanket and kissed her forehead as his father had done to him so many years ago. "Sleep well."

"Your Highness, can I tell you a secret?" she whispered.

He raised an eyebrow. He had never been privy to a little girl's secret before. He leaned close. "What is it?"

"I'm so glad you are marrying Christina, Your Highness." The seriousness of Sonia's tone surprised him. "Just between you and me, I don't think you could find anyone nicer."

Richard smiled at the way Sonia had mimicked Christina's words. "Between you and me, I think you are right."

Christina tightened her grip on the children's drawings so she wouldn't drop any of them on their way out of the hospital lobby. Thank goodness she'd worn the gloves. Thinking about Richard and the children together made her palms sweat. "You were wonderful in there."

He shrugged. "The children made it easy."

Modesty from Richard? Her image of him was changing. In a very good way. "It's more than that."

"I like children."

"That's obvious." And a total, yet welcome, surprise. She could tell Richard would take an active interest in his own children's lives and shower them with love and affection. That was the kind of man she wanted to be the father of her children. Someday... She touched the ring on her finger. "You were so patient and kind. Friendly and compassionate."

"You make it sound as if I were some kind of monster before today."

"Not a monster." She grinned. "An ogre, perhaps."

Richard laughed. "I've been called worse."

"So what were you and Sonia whispering about?"

"It is a secret. I cannot tell."

"Such loyalty to your subjects. What a valiant prince you are."

"I am sworn to secrecy. What more can I say?"

Valiant indeed. A scene of Richard and a petite little girl having a tea party flashed into Christina's mind. He would be the kind of father to relish such times with his daughter. The quickening of her pulse and her shallow breathing warned her to step back, to distance herself from the fantasy taking shape in her imagination.

Christina stepped outside and stopped. She blinked at the flashbulbs shooting off like fireworks. The lights, the cameras, the crowd. "Oh, my..."

Richard ran into her back. "What's...?"

A horde of reporters began shouting questions. More bulbs flashed. The lights blinded her. "What are we going to do?"

Richard placed his arm around her shoulders and drew her close, offering security, comfort and strength. Fighting the urge to lean into him, she looked up, silently pleading for Richard to make the noisy crowd go away. "We are stuck and will have to make the best of it."

Maybe he could. She wasn't sure she could. Christina clutched the drawings to her chest.

Richard raised his hand in the air to quiet the rapid fire of questions from the media. "Christina and I will be happy to pose for a few photographs."

Pose? She didn't want her picture taken. Not after the photograph in the newspaper this morning. Every one of her muscles tensed. Richard gave her a reassuring squeeze.

"Can you handle this?" he whispered.

"Do I have a choice?"

"No."

The way he waited for her reply, his gaze never straying from her, made her feel as if she were the only woman on Earth and he the only man. "I'll try."

"That is my Christina." He turned his attention to the reporters. "We cannot stay long, but we will answer a few questions."

"Where are you going on your honeymoon, Your Highness?"

Richard smiled. "If you were me, would you tell?"

The reporter who asked the question laughed. "Not if my life depended on it."

"That is why I am keeping it a secret. Not even Christina knows."

"Is that true, Miss Armstrong?" another reporter asked.

"Y-y-yes." Several people scribbled notes or held up microcassette recorders. "Prince Richard is good at keeping secrets."

"Is it true Delia is designing your gown, Miss Armstrong?"

Feeling out of her element, Christina hesitated. She wasn't used to direct questions. Most of her media coverage came from insider information or gossip and usually had been greatly exaggerated, making whatever faux pas she'd committed seem much worse than it was. "Y-yes, she is."

"Can you give us a description of it?"

"Not with him standing here." She pointed to Richard, whose smile urged her on. The tension evaporated from her shoulders. "In America, we have a saying that it's bad luck for the groom to see the bride in her wedding gown. Call me superstitious, but I don't want to take any chances."

Several of the crowd laughed.

"Miss Armstrong, have you decided what will be your favored charity?"

Christina didn't understand the question and glanced at Richard. He whispered, "Each de Thierry princess chooses a favorite charity and becomes its sponsor and patroness."

She smiled at the reporter who asked the question. "Am I only allowed one?"

The reporter smiled back and wrote furiously. More questions were shouted, but Christina didn't have any problem giving quotable answers.

"Please." Richard raised his hand after several minutes. "We must return to the palace. An official statement will be released shortly."

The crowd groaned.

"I know you are anxious for details, but I hope you will respect our privacy. This is a...special time for us." To Christina's amazement, several of the media nodded. Richard had handled them so deftly. "If you need any more photographs, I suggest you take them now."

With his arm still around her, they posed for a few more pictures. He turned it into a game, whispering into her ear how the media would be using these pictures and superimposing the face of his future bride once he married.

Before she knew it, they were finished. Quick and easy. More painless than she could ever have imagined. She had stood face-to-face with the media and survived.

Richard whisked her into his waiting car and closed the door. "Was that so bad?"

"No, it wasn't bad at all."

And it would be even better if Richard weren't a prince, if he would abdicate his throne and run away with her. Far away from all that was royal and visible to the outside world to a place where they could live happily ever after.

Of course, that would never happen, but Christina could spend the ten minute drive back to the palace daydreaming of a fantasy life with Richard. She rested her head against the back of the seat and sighed.

Chapter Ten

The afternoon passed with a flurry of activity. A luncheon with Princess Marguerite, a trip to the government offices to apply for a wedding license and a meeting with the bishop of San Montico, who was to perform the nuptial mass.

Wednesday arrived with anxiety. The royal wedding was approaching fast and Christina had yet to find Richard a bride. The only bright spot of the day had been when her mother called to say she was stranded at Charles de Gaulle Airport due to a workers' strike. At least something was going Christina's way.

In her suite of rooms, she pulled off her gloves, kicked off her shoes and collapsed on the sofa. She should have been combing the registry for Richard's future wife, but her heart wasn't in it.

Looking for a diversion, Christina grabbed her sketchbook from the coffee table and opened it to her drawing. After a few strokes with her pencil, the features became defined. Real. Richard.

If Prince Charming ever were to exist, he would look exactly like Richard de Thierry. Closing her eyes, she pictured every detail of his gorgeous face. His full, much-too-kissable lips, his incredible sea-blue eyes fringed with thick lashes, the determined—sometimes arrogant—set of his chin.

The lines on the paper continued to take shape. She added armor, a sword. Richard as a gallant knight astride his faithful steed, preparing to ride into battle, leaving his true love behind.

Uh-oh. What was she doing? Christina tossed her sketch book back on the table. She couldn't get wrapped up in a fairy tale. Fantasy was a long way from reality.

Reality was the flashing lights of tabloid cameras waiting to expose her latest mishap. Reality was Richard wanting to find another woman to marry. Reality was—

A knock on the door.

She hated the way her heart hoped it was Richard. "Come in."

The door opened and Didier entered. "How was your fitting?"

The frenzied pace of Delia, Elise and Faye buzzing around measuring, marking and pinning her dress reminded Christina of the "Flight of the Bumblebee." Through it all, she had to keep reminding herself that Delia's breathtaking work of art—a dress fit for a fairy princess—was something Christina would never need.

It saddened her to think all the designer's hard work was for nothing. Maybe Richard's bride would be the same size. Then again, a princess bride wouldn't want a hand-me-down gown. "The fitting went...well."

"I'm so pleased." His ear-to-ear smile affirmed his genuine pleasure. "I have a surprise for you."

Kelsey Armstrong Waters stepped into the room holding

a cat carrier. "Surprise, little cousin, look what the cat dragged in."

"Kelsey." Christina rose and gave her a big hug. "You're here and Francis, too."

"George is a great cat-sitter. He was waiting for me when I arrived at O'Hare with Francis and a copy of her medical records."

"Why did you bring her?"

"After the wedding, you'll be living here. I figured you would want Francis with you. I know how much the little fur face means to you."

As did Christina's family. They would disinherit her when they found out the truth. She didn't care about the money, but the family ties... She swallowed the lump in her throat. "Thanks. I hope it wasn't too much trouble."

"It wasn't. Francis and I flew first class. She had her own seat."

As Christina opened the carrier, she noticed the way Didier's gaze kept returning to Kelsey. No doubt he was taken in by her cover-girl looks. Most men were usually captivated by her big violet eyes, waist-length chestnut hair and vivacious smile.

Free at last, Francis scurried under the bed. Christina closed the door. "Please tell me you didn't feed her any human food?"

"Of course not." Kelsey's eyes sparkled. "But did you know she loves beluga?"

Christina glared at her cousin. "Spoiled kitty."

"She's not the only one." Kelsey whistled and her eyes widened. "So that's the ring."

"Yes." Christina held out her left hand. "The royal engagement ring."

"You could do worse. A lot worse." Kelsey grinned. "Where are your gloves?"

"How did you know about the gloves?"

Didier stepped forward. "I told Miss Waters how you've started a new fashion trend on the island."

"Me?" Christina was the least fashionable of all the Armstrongs. Preferring comfort over labels, she annually made the worst-dressed lists, much to the chagrin of her mother.

He nodded. "Every female on San Montico wants to wear them and all the shops have sold out. It's quite charming."

"I'm sure it is." Kelsey flipped her hair behind her shoulder, a casual move perfected after years of practice. "I'll have to get a pair for myself."

"If I can be of any assistance, please let me know," Didier offered.

Kelsey batted her eyelashes. "You're much too kind."

His cheeks reddened. *Another one bites the dust.*

"I'll have Francis's luggage brought in." Didier bowed and left the room.

"Her luggage?" Christina asked.

"I couldn't just wrap her litter box in a garbage bag and carry it onto the plane and into the palace. Besides, she has so many furry mice and other toys. Luggage was a necessity."

"You are too much."

"Enough about the fur ball." Kelsey wet her lips. "Let's talk about Didier. Isn't he positively dreamy? So handsome and polite and nice. And I just love the way he calls me 'Miss Waters.' I wonder if he's married. I didn't see a ring. Do you think you could find out for me?"

Love-'em-and-leave-'em Kelsey. She got bored after the second date. Poor Didier. He would never know what hit him. "I'll try."

"I knew I could count on you." Kelsey glanced around the room, taking in the sitting area and fireplace, the writing desk and the bed. "A tad on the provincial side, but tasteful."

"You should see Richard's room."

"Richard's?" Kelsey plopped on the sofa and patted the seat next to her. "I want to know about all the mouthwatering kisses and heated caresses and steamy sex."

Leave it to Kelsey to blow things out of proportion. Christina sighed. "When have I ever had a steamy sex story to tell?"

"A girl can hope, can't she?" Kelsey raised one of her finely arched brows. "So start at the beginning and don't leave out a single detail." When Christina finished explaining the situation, Kelsey rose. "I don't get it. A handsome prince, a gorgeous palace, a magical love spell. I'd be thinking happily ever after if I were you. Are you sure you know what you're doing?"

Christina nodded. "The legend doesn't mean anything."

"It means everything, and you know it, too." Kelsey wagged her finger. "You're wearing the ring. He has to marry you."

"No, he doesn't." Christina sounded like a broken record. Someday she would look back and cry—no laugh. "Since when have you become a proponent of marriage?"

"I'll admit the institution of marriage is not for me, but it's perfect for you and thousands of others." Kelsey glanced at the sketchbook lying open on the coffee table. "You've fallen for him, haven't you?"

Christina stared at her lap. Since meeting Richard, she'd been fighting her growing attraction. Every time he was near her, something happened. Her nerve endings tingled with anticipation. Her stomach did cartwheels, but seeing him with the children had melted a piece of her heart.

She saw beyond His Serene Highness's princely exterior to the real man underneath, and to her surprise she liked what she saw. A man who was untouchable but wanted to be touched. A man who was unconquerable but needed to be conquered. A man who was loving but pretended not to love.

He might think his heart was encased in armor, but he was wrong. Magic might not penetrate it, but love would. Someday he would see that for himself.

But she couldn't believe in a happy ending for this fairy tale. Happily ever after wouldn't happen for her and Richard.

She wanted a man whose family would be his priority, who would always be there for them and not at a prestigious job, who would always have time to share and love to give, a man who was ordinary. Richard was none—okay, maybe a few of those things, but he wasn't ordinary. He ruled an island and would always live his life in the public eye. "He's everything I don't want in a man."

"Still hoping for a home on the range?"

"I thought so...." Christina shook off her uncertainty.

Kelsey took her hand. "You need to think long and hard about what you're doing. You won't get a second chance."

"I know. I—"

I love him.

Oh, no. Christina closed her eyes, realizing it was true. She had fallen for him, fallen hard. But she didn't want him to "have to" marry her; she wanted him to "want to" marry her.

She stared at the ring and remembered.

Only true love could remove it.

She pulled on the gold band. Hard. The ring didn't budge.

Unrequited love didn't count.

The ring may have worked its magic on her, but the enchanted spell hadn't worked with Richard. She could never marry a man who didn't love her as much as she loved him. No matter how strong her feelings might be.

Christina buried her head in her hands. "How could I be so stupid?"

"You're not stupid." Kelsey gave her a big hug full of warmth. "And it's not the end of the world. Aunt Claire will never recover, but *you* will get over this."

Of course she would, Christina rationalized. She hadn't found a once-in-a-lifetime love. She'd simply gotten caught up in the wonder and enchantment of the legend.

Just like everyone else at the palace.

Just like everyone else in San Montico.

Everyone, except Richard.

Dinner was a lavish affair with most of the Armstrong family in attendance. Richard could not wait until it was over. He missed speaking with Christina. Her family was monopolizing all her time, leaving him to deal with his family's honeymoon suggestions. As soon as dessert was finished, he excused both himself and Christina and escorted her to her room.

He tried to understand the mixture of emotions churning within him. Relief at having escaped the crowd downstairs and finally having Christina all to himself, and confusion at seeing her enthusiasm to get back to work and find him a wife. Odd feelings given the circumstances.

Sitting at her desk with a peerage registry opened, Christina stuck her pen behind her ear. "I'm so happy dinner is over with."

"Your cousins were quite attentive."

"Of course. Now they care whether I'm around or not. That'll change as soon as our engagement is off."

"Does that bother you?"

"Not as much as I thought it would," she admitted. "I can't live my life trying to please my family. I realize that now. If all of San Montico can accept me because I wear the ring, my family can accept me when I'm no longer wearing it." Christina grinned. "Maybe there is something magical about this ring. I don't mean a love spell, but do you realize how long it's been without an accident, an incident or a mishap occurring?"

"Coincidence."

She drew her brows together, and two little lines appeared above the bridge of her nose. "Don't spoil it, okay?"

"Okay." He noticed a furry cat tail sticking out from under the bed skirt. "How is Francis adjusting?"

"I wish I could chalk it up to jet lag, but she's been a handful today."

Richard knelt and lifted the bed skirt. "Francis, come here."

The cat scooted farther underneath the bed, gave him the evil eye and hissed.

"She doesn't understand about following royal orders."

"Apparently not." He stood. "I only wanted to see what she looked like."

"You will. In a couple of days, she'll be prancing around this place as if she were queen of the castle."

But they did not have a couple of days. Time was running out, and they both knew it. His gaze met hers. "Any new possibilities?"

"No. Did you check the names on the last list?"

He nodded. "One is climbing in the Alps, another is already engaged, the other has joined a religious order."

Christina pointed to the peerage registry. She wasn't wearing her gloves. "I only have five letters left—V, W, X, Y and Z."

He glanced at her bare hand. The engagement ring twinkled beneath the lights, almost mocking him. "Maybe we shall get lucky."

"And if we don't? What's our backup plan?"

"I do not have one. How about you?"

She frowned. "I've had my nose buried too deep in these books to think of anything else. Coming up with a list of eligible candidates has not been an easy task."

"Now you know what the past six months have been like for me."

She nodded, her eyes full of understanding.

"What if we find you a husband? That might be easier." The suggestion left a funny feeling in the pit of his stomach. "I could round up a bunch of cowboys and let you choose—"

"I'll find my own husband, thank you very much."

He shrugged. "It was worth a try."

"Do you know what your mother said to me today?"

He could only imagine. "What?"

"She said I was the best daughter-in-law she could hope to have. And your uncle, he..." She stared at the book on the desk but didn't seem to be looking at the registry. "It's just...I haven't even married into your family, but they've been kinder and more accepting than my own family. It's been really nice."

Richard touched her shoulder. "One day you will have your own family who will be everything you dream about."

"I know." She sighed. "I'll finish going through the registry, you come up with a Plan B and we'll meet later."

"Plan B?"

"A backup plan. We need one, you know. In case we can't find you another woman to marry." She pulled her pen from behind her ear. "Good luck."

"You, too."

Richard returned to his room—his sanctuary—but tonight the only thing within these walls was a feeling of loneliness. Staring at the flames in the fireplace, he tried to think of a backup plan, but his thoughts kept straying to Christina.

Perhaps he was beginning to care for her. After all they

had been through in such a short time, it would be difficult not to feel a slight affection for her. But he could not afford to feel anything more. Anything more meant accepting the Legend of the Ring, meant risking his heart and soul in the pursuit of...true love.

He did not want to fall in love. He was still hurting from Thea's betrayal. He did not want to feel that pain, that sting of rejection, but it was more than that. Women were attracted to him because he was a prince. Thea had been neither the first nor the last. He was used to it. But Christina was different. She did not want him because he *was* a prince.

What was he going to do?

First and foremost, he could not lose his throne. That had to be his main, his only, priority. He could not let his family's reign over San Montico end, nor could he break his promise to his father. Losing the throne meant losing everything.

Richard must wed.

But whom?

Christina. She was the logical choice, given the lack of other worthy candidates. Marrying her would keep the legend alive, but it would keep him from abdicating. After the wedding, he would have time to prove the legend untrue, prove that the ring had not found his true love. He would get the marriage annulled and remarry a woman of his own choosing. In the end, he would keep both his throne and his heart intact.

This would be his Plan B.

But how could he get Christina to marry him? She wanted to marry a man she loved. What he needed was...

Magic.

If only he could believe.

Desperate, Richard picked up the telephone. He could not do this; he did not believe in magic. He went to place the receiver back in its cradle, then stopped himself. His throne was on the line. Something had to be done, however selfish and underhanded.

Vowing to use it only as a last resort, he dialed the number. A groggy voice answered on the other end. Richard clutched the phone. "I am sorry to wake you, but it is important."

"Your Highness?"

"Yes." It was insane to think magic would work, but what choice did he have? "Merlin, I need that love potion after all."

Thanks to the secret tunnels, Richard sneaked out of the palace. Following his visit to Merlin's cottage, Richard slipped back in without being noticed. As he walked down the hallway to his room, he saw Christina sitting on the floor, leaning against one of his doors. "What are you doing out here?"

She rose and brushed her palms on the legs of her pants. "I've been waiting for you."

"I had an errand to run." Why had he said that? He didn't need to explain his comings and goings to her.

"An errand?"

He nodded. The errand threatened to burn a hole in his pocket if he was not more careful. Perhaps her presence was a sign to proceed with his plan. "Would you care to come in for a drink?"

"I'd love to. I could really use a drink."

The circles under her tired eyes told the tale. "The search is getting to you."

"A little, but I finished going through the registries." She did not sound hopeful. "I—"

"Shall we have that drink first?" Inside his room, he opened a cabinet that hid a bar from sight, pulled out a crystal decanter and poured a healthy amount of brandy into two snifters. On purpose, he splashed a drop of the amber liquid on the bar top and one of the glasses. "Would you please get me a towel from the bathroom?"

"Sure."

As Christina retrieved a towel, Richard opened a small cobalt-blue tube containing love potion No. 23. *Guaranteed results or his money back.* Richard sniffed the liquid inside the glass vial. No scent. He hesitated.

Should he use it?

He could not abdicate. He could not find another bride. That left Christina. Her exhaustive search had showed him she would not marry him willingly. Her sketch told him she was holding out for a cowboy, however unlikely that fantasy of hers might be. And her vow to only marry a man she loved gave him no other choice.

The potion was his only hope.

Richard reminded himself that his decision had nothing to with any feelings he might have for Christina, but everything to do with practicality. He emptied the vial into her drink and swirled the snifter, mixing the clear potion with the brandy.

It was done.

Christina returned to the room and handed him the towel. He wiped the top of the bar, patted the edge of one of the glasses and gave it to her. She held the drink in her palm.

His heart rate increased as it always did at the start of a sailing regatta, but this was more important than any race. This was life...his.

"A toast." She raised her glass. "To your future wife."

Wife? Did she mean herself or had she found...?

His heart plummeted. He had to stop her from drinking the potion. Richard took a step toward her. She lifted the snifter to her mouth and sipped. He knocked the glass out of her hand. Amber liquid splashed out of the tumbling glass. The snifter hit the floor with a thud, but did not break. Brandy soaked the rug.

Christina's eyes widened. "What did you do that for?"

"Did you drink any?"

She used the towel from the bar to wipe up the spill. "A little, before you—"

"How much?"

"A sip." Christina placed the towel and her empty glass on the table. "I'm not in the habit of chugging brandy."

Perhaps only a sip would not work. For her sake, he hoped so. "Would you like another drink?"

"Uh, no. I'll pass, thanks." She sat in one of the reading chairs in front of the fireplace. "Is something wrong?"

"No, not at all." Richard sat in the other chair so he had a good view of Christina. He wasn't sure what to expect if the potion started to work. "So about this woman."

Christina licked her lips and stared at the carpet. "Princess Julianna Von Schneckle of Aliestle."

"Aliestle?" Richard nearly dropped his own glass. "Our two countries have not spoken for over—"

"One hundred and thirty-nine years," Christina offered. "I looked it up."

"I do not care how long it has been. I could never marry an Aliestlian." He downed his brandy. "My people would never accept her as their princess."

"Of course they would." Christina fiddled with the ring. "Your marriage to Princess Julianna would resolve your dispute and reunite the two countries."

He rose, clasped his hands behind his back and paced. "I want a marriage, not a treaty."

"You don't plan to marry for love anyway, so why should it matter?"

She made his marriage sound so businesslike, unappealing. He kept pacing. Back and forth. Back and forth across the room. He could not marry Princess Julianna. Perhaps

Christina had drunk enough of the potion, and it just needed time to work its magic. Anything not to marry an Aliestlian.

"Would you sit down and relax for a minute? It's like watching a tennis match. My neck is starting to hurt."

He sat and tapped his foot. "This is not going to work."

She frowned. "You want to marry a woman of your own choosing, not one chosen by the legend. Princess Julianna Von Schneckle is twenty-five and meets all the qualifications on your list. The least you can do is speak with her."

Why wasn't the potion working? Surely Christina should be acting flirtatiously, gazing coyly, batting her eyelashes, throwing herself at him by now. Richard rubbed his chin. "Every one?"

She nodded. "Did I mention to you that Princess Julianna is an accomplished sailor, too?"

"She sails? You spoke with her?"

"We're running out of time. I thought it only fair to explain the situation. She was understanding and helpful. I...liked her."

She liked her? Christina should not like her even if the princess sailed. She should be pining away for him, declaring her undying love, begging him to marry her, not some unknown princess from a backward European country.

"Every official I spoke with at the Aliestlian castle was nice. I think you'll like your in-laws."

"I do not want to like them," he admitted. "Perhaps we should try removing the ring again. Maybe it will come off and we—"

"It's not coming off." She took a deep breath and exhaled slowly.

Of course it wasn't. If Christina loved him, she would try to remove the ring. And if he loved her...

"Don't sit there frowning. Princess Julianna will be good for you and San Montico."

"She is from Aliestle."

"For someone who wants to bring his country into the modern age, you sure are stuck in the past, holding on to some antiquated belief that says you hate all Aliestlians."

"I am not."

"Yes, you are."

She did not know what she was saying. A few days on the island—his island—did not make her an expert on his own people.

"You speak of doing away with all the legends and customs that give your country character, yet you keep this aristocratic Hatfield-McCoy feud alive and cling to the most outdated mind-set of them all—the monarchy. You're a…hypocrite."

Obviously, he had been right all along. Magic did not exist. He would ask Merlin for a full refund. Richard sighed.

Her eyes narrowed. "You condemn your own people for living in the Dark Ages, while you cling to royal protocol, *Your Highness*. If you wanted true modernization, you should abolish the monarchy. Treat every citizen as an equal. But you don't want that. You want to change everything except what works for you."

She planted her hands on her hips. "But you know what, *Your Highness?* You'd better get over it. You either marry Princess Julianna or…"

You. "Or?"

"Abdicate."

Chapter Eleven

The next morning, Christina sat in the salon drumming her gloved fingers on the settee. She'd been waiting for hours.

Richard and the Royal Council were meeting with members of the Aliestle royal family and the Aliestle Council of Elders. Unless they resolved their century-long dispute, King Alaric of Aliestle had proclaimed that no marriage discussions could take place. Both the council and the elders, however, believed Christina wanted Princess Julianna, an "old" friend, to be a bridesmaid.

Yawning, Christina fought her tiredness. Sleep had not come last night, and she was paying the price today. But come tomorrow, she would have plenty of time to sleep. Plenty of time to do whatever she wanted to do. Plenty of time to mend her broken heart.

The salon doors swung open, and Didier stepped inside. "His Royal Highness Crown Prince Brandt Roland Wilhelm of Aliestle and Her Royal Highness Princess Julianna Louise Marie."

Christina stood. A man and woman entered the room, followed by Richard. Didier closed the salon doors on his way out.

Princess Julianna was everything Richard could want in a wife—beautiful, elegant, stylish. In her sleeveless royal-blue dress, the princess made Christina feel like an out-of-shape bag lady. Prince Brandt was handsome, as dark as his sister was fair, but his exterior ruggedness didn't match his refined movements and dress. He would look perfect in the suit of armor on display in the Great Hall.

Richard wore a tailored navy suit, white dress shirt and coordinating silk tie. The regal way he carried himself made him look more like a prince than ever before, but the tight line of his lips made her wonder how the negotiations had gone. "Your Highnesses, may I introduce Miss Christina Armstrong from the United States of America."

Christina curtsied.

Prince Brandt took her hand, raised it to his lips and kissed it. Just as Richard had—minus the glove—the night of his birthday ball. "It is an honor to meet you, Miss Armstrong."

His approving gaze raked over her, and Christina felt her cheeks warm.

"It is a pleasure to meet you in person, Miss Armstrong," Princess Julianna said politely. "I enjoyed our telephone conversation."

"Thank you, Your Highness. I appreciate you coming so quickly."

Princess Julianna tilted her chin. "After your desperate phone call, I didn't want to waste a single moment."

Richard shot Christina a pointed look. "Desperate?"

Christina merely shrugged, but she had been desperate. She had wanted to find him a woman worthy of all he had to give, a woman who would be good not only for him, but San Montico. A woman who could give Richard the love she knew he deserved.

"Well, I'm here now," Princess Julianna stated. "Your desperate times are over."

Not really. Christina's were only beginning, but that was another story.

Tea arrived and the four of them sat. Political talk about uniting San Montico and Aliestle dragged on, and tension filled the air despite the civil conversation.

Raising her teacup to her lips, Christina stared over the rim at Richard. She got the feeling things hadn't gone well at the meeting. Not only the two countries, but Richard and Julianna had to resolve matters if they were to marry tomorrow. "How did the negotiations go, Your Highnesses?"

Prince Brandt motioned for Richard to proceed. "We have decided to share equal responsibility for the disagreement. A document is being drawn up by the council and elders."

"What wonderful news." Only Christina didn't see any pleasure on the others' faces. "Isn't it?"

Princess Julianna smiled. "Yes, it is wonderful news. Forgive us for not sharing in the excitement, Miss Armstrong, but the meeting was quite...taxing."

"I'm sure it was, but if your disagreement is water under the bridge, why don't we stop all this political chitchat and start talking about what's really important—the royal wedding?"

Everyone laughed, and the tension eased.

"And I hope, Your Highnesses, you will feel comfortable calling me Christina."

Prince Brandt's grin made him look like a little boy let loose in a candy store. "Thank you, Christina."

"Don't mind my brother," Princess Julianna said. "He's a terrible flirt."

"I must plead guilty as charged, but I have a good reason." Prince Brandt sighed. "You see, my own fate was sealed when I was twelve and betrothed to the daughter of our ambassador to America. I've met her once. Imagine growing up with the only image of your bride as a chubby eight-year-old who wears bottle-thick glasses and loves chocolate éclairs. You would be a flirt, too."

Richard smiled. "Completely understandable due to the circumstances."

Prince Brandt nodded. "What I wouldn't give to have a ring that would find my true love."

"If I could give it to you, I would," Richard said, and the two princes shared a knowing look. The men might have been from different countries, but they had more in common than they realized.

"Arranged marriages are the tradition in Aliestle," Princess Julianna explained to Christina. "Most are contracted when we are children. My match was made when I was only seven."

"Your match?" Christina asked.

"My former match." The light in Julianna's eyes dimmed. "He was deemed unacceptable years ago." Her smile vanished then reappeared, and she chuckled. "I'm sorry, I should have told you that first."

The princess might joke about her childhood match, but she was still in love. Christina recognized the symptoms because she knew them all too well herself.

As the conversation continued, she waited for Richard to excuse her so he could be alone with Julianna and discuss the marriage arrangements, but he didn't. And Christina did not want to stay. Imagining his and Julianna's future together... It was more than Christina could take.

She set her nearly full teacup on the tray and stood. "I'm not sure of protocol, but I would be happy to show Prince

Brandt around the palace grounds if you would like some…privacy.''

"That's a splendid idea." Prince Brandt rose. "Would you mind, Jules? Your Highness?''

Richard hesitated. ''I…''

Julianna glanced at him. ''Your Highness?''

"Yes, go," Richard said. "Prince Brandt might enjoy the challenge of the maze.''

"Thank you, Your Highness." Julianna stared at her brother. "Be good.''

Prince Brandt's smile widened. ''I'm always good.''

Julianna sighed. "That's what I'm afraid of.''

Richard frowned. ''Maybe—''

"We'll see you later." Christina wished she could dislike Julianna, but she couldn't. It wasn't the princess's fault she was everything Richard wanted. But Christina didn't understand why he looked so unhappy. He was getting everything he wanted. She was the one getting nothing.

Except a broken heart.

Having tea and talking with Julianna proved one thing. She was as perfect as Christina had said. Julianna met every requirement on his list and had made a strong impression on him. She would make a wonderful princess and be an asset to San Montico. The marriage would unite their two countries and prove the legend wrong. He would be able to lead San Montico toward change and progress as his father had desired.

All Richard's problems would be solved.

All but one.

She was not the woman he wanted to spend the rest of his life with. She did not have freckles, nor did two little lines form above the bridge of her nose when she got serious. She did not spill or break things and laugh at her mishaps. He would hazard a guess she had never set fire to anything except for the hearts of admiring men. And she had not spent all her time searching for another woman to marry him.

Logically, none of those things should matter. He should marry Julianna. She was the right choice, the best choice for him and the perfect choice for his country.

But even though he was choosing to marry her, Julianna was no different from the rest of the women he had known. She was marrying him because he was a prince. Their marriage might turn out to be a happy union and in time love might grow between them, but it *was* nothing more than a business arrangement, a merger of two countries.

Only one woman saw beyond his royal title.

Only one woman saw him first as a man, then as a prince.

Only Christina.

Like a spinnaker sail waiting to fill and race downwind, Richard, too, was ready to head toward his own finish line. But this was not a race. More was at stake than a gold cup and bragging rights. And this wasn't only about him, but two countries with a bloody past.

"Your Highness..." Richard hesitated. "How do you feel about our...match?"

"It would be beneficial to our countries."

"Yes, it would, but how do *you* feel?"

She took a deep breath. "I..."

"Did your family force you into coming?"

"'Force' is such a strong word," she said. "I was encouraged to come. As the eldest in our family, I am responsible for setting a good example for my brothers. I do what is required of me."

As should I. Richard stared at her. "Is a match between us what you want?"

She gazed into her teacup. "I must admit I would not be heartbroken if the arrangement between us did not happen."

He exhaled a breath he did not realize he had been holding, relieved that she had her own doubts, too. "Truly?"

"I have always wanted to marry for love. Even with the Aliestlian custom of arranged marriages, I thought it could happen." She sighed. "Maybe someday it will, and I will find a man who loves me the way you love Christina."

Richard stiffened. "Love Christina?"

"Don't look so shocked." Julianna smiled. "Remember I have four younger brothers."

"I do not know what to say." Opening himself up to the possibility meant risking everything he held dear—his family, his throne, his country—but he didn't have a choice. Even if it meant rejection. Even if it meant heartbreak. Even if it meant war. "You are not offended?"

"Perhaps a little," Julianna admitted. "But I'll take comfort with the knowledge I'm one of the first Aliestlians alive who have set foot on San Montico soil, let alone had tea at the palace with the ruling prince. That should assure my place in the history books and make my other brothers extremely jealous. And I would hate to stand in the way of the legend."

"Ah, yes. The legend."

Was it time to stop running and admit the truth? He couldn't pick and choose what his people should believe. Some traditions were truly antiquated and held San Montico back, but others enriched the culture and made the island a special place to live. He was trying too hard to remain in control, make all the correct choices. He was missing out on life...and love. He had been so stubborn, refusing to believe the Legend of the Ring, that he could not see the precious gift he'd been given.

Christina.

Julianna arched a delicate brow. "Christina's feelings for you are as strong as yours are for her."

"I wish that were true."

"Men," Julianna muttered. She removed a piece of paper from her purse and unfolded it. "Any woman would be able to look at this and see that Christina cares for you…deeply."

Richard studied the paper—a copy of Christina's sketch. Only it was not a drawing of a cowboy. It was…him, wearing a suit of armor and riding a horse. He held a sword in one hand and a helmet in the other. "Where did you get this?"

"Christina faxed it to me last night. No pictures of the de Thierry royal family are allowed in Aliestle, and I wanted to know what you looked like. This was the only one she had." Julianna handed him the sheet of paper. "Christina's quite a talented artist."

Her talent was only the first of her many wonderful qualities. As he stared at the drawing, Richard realized he was on the precipice of something new, something wonderful. He could sense it; he could feel it. The legend might have found Christina, but in the end he chose her himself. And he did not intend to let her go without a fight, no matter what the consequence. "Yes, she is."

Julianna smiled. "I wish you all the happiness in the world."

"I wish I could repay you somehow."

"Actually, you can." She placed her hand on his shoulder. "Bring Christina to Aliestle for your honeymoon. We may not unite our countries with our marriage, but we can unite them with our friendship."

A born diplomat. It was unfortunate Julianna would not be the one to rule her country. Aliestlians would be hard-pressed to find a ruler who cared more than she did. "Thank you."

Julianna nodded. Her lovely and serene smile would look beautiful in a royal portrait. "Perhaps you would allow us to stay until tomorrow?"

"Certainly."

"Wonderful." Beaming, she clasped her hands together. "I just love weddings."

Christina stood on the raised center of the maze with Prince Brandt by her side. She gazed past the palace grounds and over an endless sapphire sea to the horizon. If she listened hard enough, she could hear the waves of the Mediterranean crashing against the shore. She wanted to capture the sound in her heart and take the memory home with her.

"What an incredible view," Prince Brandt said.

"Yes, it's spectacular." She would miss not only the view, but all of San Montico. The warm breeze, carrying the scent of the sea, brushed her skin. To her right, narrow stone streets weaved their way through the colorful buildings of the village perched on the hillside. The spires of the cathedral jutted into the cloudless azure sky, completing the scene. Picture postcard perfect. Like a fairy tale.

Only it wasn't her fairy tale—the one where she married the prince and lived happily ever after. And, Christina realized with a shock, that was okay.

Her visit to San Montico had taught her so much.

She would always have the memories of her time at the palace and with Richard, but more importantly, she would return home a changed woman.

When the news about Richard's marriage to Julianna broke, Christina's family would consider her more of a failure than ever before. But she didn't care. Not the way she used to care. She had finally realized it was their problem, not hers. Marrying a prince—or not marrying him—had nothing to do with her and who she was inside.

And if the media wanted to use her for their fun, so be it. She would use them in return and bring those things she held near and dear to her heart—animals and children—

with her to the spotlight. She would stop hiding behind a canvas and live without worrying about the repercussions and headlines.

She might choose to move out west and live an ordinary life, but it was her choice to do so, not a necessity. And to be honest, she wasn't even sure what defined "ordinary."

Maybe one of these days, if she still wanted to, she would find out.

"You'll have to visit Aliestle." Prince Brandt smiled. "We have some spectacular views ourselves."

"I'm sure you do, but I must admit I'm partial to this one." She hugged her stomach. She would never be able to forget him....

Christina felt rather than heard Richard step behind her. He placed his hands on her shoulders. His light touch gave her a sense of expectancy, something weightless, buoyant. It was almost magical, but not even magic could help her now. "Where's Princess Julianna?"

"Inside," he said. "Prince Brandt, she asked that you join her. My advisor, Didier, is waiting at the bottom of the maze and will escort you."

"Thank you for the tour, Christina." Prince Brandt made a slight bow and left.

It took all Christina's willpower to break the contact of Richard's soft touch and face him. She didn't want to ask but forced the words from her lips. "How did it go?"

A mysterious smiled graced his lips. "Fine."

She waited for him to tell her more, but he didn't. "So?"

"I enjoyed speaking with her. You were correct. Julianna meets every one of my requirements."

Christina never thought hearing the truth from his lips would hurt as much as it did. She smiled only to keep her own from trembling. "Good."

"Julianna is beautiful."

Christina nodded. No one would dare disagree with that.

"She adores children."

So do I. Not that it mattered, Christina reminded herself for the umpteenth time. She had finally done something right; she had found Richard a wife. She should be happy for him and his new fiancée. Someday she would look back...

"And wants lots of them."

Me, too. Christina might not have blue blood, but she couldn't help but think she was as qualified as Julianna to be Richard's wife. If only he could see it.

"She has her master's degree."

Okay, the princess had a brain to match her body, but having a master's degree wasn't everything. He was slipping away from her, and there was nothing she could do to stop it. Christina shouldn't care. She didn't want to be a princess and live in a palace.

"She speaks German, French, English and Italian."

I speak three of the four. Christina fought the urge to scream the words at him even though she knew they would do no good. He already knew that. She wanted to cry.

"But..."

She looked at him. "But what?"

"She is allergic to cats."

Christina frowned. "You don't have any cats and that was not one of your requirements."

Richard shrugged. "Still, I do not want to marry her."

"You...what?" Surely she hadn't heard him correctly.

"I do not wish to marry her."

"But...I don't understand. Julianna meets all the requirements on your list. She's perfect."

"I know, but something is...missing."

Christina couldn't believe this. After what he'd put her through... She glanced toward heaven. "What's missing is your brain."

"I can explain."

"Explain what? You're the one who wanted to make a choice, to prove the legend wrong."

He reached for her. "Christina—"

She brushed him off. "No, I don't want to hear anything you have to say. I don't care if you are a prince. You have no right to do this. I work my tail off to find you a woman who meets all your stupid qualifications and you have the nerve to tell me something is missing? Well, I've had it. You run from the legend as if it's the plague. You're not only a hypocrite, you're a scaredy-cat."

"A scaredy-cat?"

"If the shoe fits…"

"Are you finished?"

"No. I'm not. Don't you see, Richard?" She wanted to shake him. "It's not only the legend you're afraid of, but love. A lifetime of happiness, joy and love is waiting for you, but you're afraid to go for it." She realized her words could describe herself as well as Richard, but she couldn't worry about that right now. "So your heart was broken once. Thea was a fool for ever letting you go. Don't give her the power to ruin everything for you."

"Are you finished now?"

She crossed her arms over her chest and nodded.

He took a deep breath. "I am not afraid to 'go for it.' Maybe I was afraid of falling in love, but only because I have experienced the pain of loving and losing. Facing rejection is not easy when everything else in life has come so easily. And I have seen the grief my mother has suffered these ten long years."

"No one said love was ever easy or painless, but the rewards are so worth it. If you ask your mother, she'll tell you she doesn't regret one moment of her life with your father."

"I…know." He looked away. "They were so happy."

"And you can be, too." It broke Christina's heart to say

the words, to push him into the arms of another woman, but she had no choice. This was for Richard's own good. She had to be strong.

"When I saw you with Prince Brandt, I thought of Thea and King Gustav."

"Oh, please, spare me." Christina grimaced. "I was only showing him the view. He's a terrible flirt, but nothing happened. You can't compare me to Thea."

"No, I cannot and that is what I realized." Richard stared into Christina's eyes. "There is no comparison. I trust you implicitly."

The air whooshed out of her lungs. "Y-y-you do?"

He nodded. "I admit when I first met you, I thought you were just like her. Nothing more than a title-seeking American."

"I am an American."

"Yes, but I was judging you the same way others have judged me. I could not see beyond your being an heiress from America. I am as guilty of stereotyping you as all those women who see me as a prince and nothing more. As if we are all alike. I know you have nothing in common with Thea except your nationality." Richard winked and flashed his most charming grin, dimple and all. "Now if Prince Brandt were named Tex or Jake and wore a cowboy hat and boots, I might have been a little concerned."

The pitter-pat of Christina's heart made her think Richard was flirting, and his trust in her meant more than she could say. She wanted to tell him everything he'd come to mean to her. If only... She looked away. "I don't see what any of this has to do with you and Julianna."

"It has everything to do with—"

"You must marry, Richard."

"I know that."

"Please, there's no other way."

"I know that, too."

"If you don't, you'll lose the throne."

"That is not going to happen."

"I couldn't bear it if you—"

"Marry me, Christina."

"Marry Julianna."

"What?" they asked at the same time.

He smiled. "Will you marry me, Christina?"

"Me? Marry you?" Her mind went blank. All rational thought vanished. If not for the sound of her breathing, she would have thought her heart stopped beating. She stood frozen, unable to move, to speak, to blink.

This wasn't happening. She had to be dreaming. Any moment Francis would rub against her cheek and Christina would wake up. She waited a full minute. Nothing changed. Richard continued to watch her anxiously. She was struck by the image of him as a young boy asking Princess Marguerite if he could hold one of the magnificent swords displayed on the palace walls and nervously awaiting her answer.

What was Richard thinking? There must be a logical reason for his wanting to marry her. Some reason to make him want... Christina raised her chin, aware it was shaking. "It's the ring. You're worried about the ring. I'd rather chop off my finger—"

"There will be no chopping of fingers." He sighed and brushed his hand through his hair. "I am going about this all wrong."

"What are you—"

"I want to show you something." He grabbed her hand. "Come with me."

She followed him through a trapdoor at the center of the maze, down a circular staircase to a tunnel. The air felt thick and heavy and smelled musty. Her eyes adjusted to the darkness.

Something wet hit her forehead. Christina glanced up.

Water dripped from a pipe above. She passed an old steam generator, its parts rusted and covered in dust and cobwebs. Richard climbed another circular staircase and opened a door. Daylight. Christina blinked.

The smells of hay and horses and the sounds of hooves and neighing filled the air. They were at the stables.

Richard took a deep breath, and Christina prepared herself for the worst. She simply couldn't believe...

"I do not want Julianna." He took Christina's hand in his. "I want you."

A lump the size of Montana lodged in her throat.

"I am not a cowboy with a ranch and cattle, but I have this stable with some of the most beautiful horses in the world. I am not a farmer with a hundred-year-old farmhouse and acres of crops, but I have an island with acres of fertile land. I am not a mechanic with grease under my fingernails, but I know how to fix a flat tire.

"I am not your everyday average guy. I do not know if I can be one. But if you marry me, I will do my best to make your life as ordinary as you'd like."

Christina blinked back tears. "Oh, Richard, you would really choose me over Princess Julianna?"

"In a heartbeat."

"You don't know how much that means to me."

"It does?" His eyes widened, hope warring with skepticism in their depths. "Then why did you work so hard to find me a wife?"

"B-both you and I agreed I wasn't princess material."

"I do not say it often, but I will say it now. I was wrong. More wrong than I have ever been in my life. I want you, Christina." The words tumbled from his lips. The eager look in his eyes, on his face, showed his sincerity. "Only you."

She covered her mouth with both hands. If this were a dream, she didn't want to wake up. Ever.

"You are the most amazing woman I have ever known. Beautiful, caring, generous, talented. You fill a part of me I did not even know was missing. The way you forget about royal protocol... I never realized I could like that, but I do. And when you say my name... You are the only woman besides my mother who sees me for who I am. Not a prince, but a man. You satisfy me in a way I never imagined possible."

Tears clung to her eyelashes, and it was too late to blink them away. "What about my klutziness? I wouldn't want to put you or the palace or San Montico at risk."

"Your so-called klutziness is one of your most endearing traits."

She wanted so badly to believe what he said was true. "I'd hate to...embarrass you."

"You could never do that, Christina. Never." He smoothed her hair with his hand. "Remember what you said last night about not having any accidents or mishaps?"

She nodded. He had said it was a coincidence.

"It has been another sixteen hours or so. The ring seems to have worked its magic as you said."

"Magic?"

"Yes, magic."

"But what if it hasn't? What if—"

"I will take whatever precautions I need to take. Install sprinklers throughout the palace if I must." Richard smiled, taking her breath away once again. "I love everything about you and that includes your accidents, incidents and whatever minor insurrections you have caused or will cause in the future. I do not care about those things. I care only about you."

All the words he was saying were so right, so perfect. Her heart pounded as fast as a pair of hummingbird wings. She was struggling not to throw herself into his arms and kiss him until there wasn't an ounce of air left to breathe.

But she couldn't. Not until she heard him say the three words she needed to hear.

"I love you, Christina." Richard kissed her lightly on the lips, and it was all she could do not to swoon. "I will always love you no matter what you do and perhaps in time you will grow to love me. I want the kind of marriage my parents had."

"But I—"

"Before you say anything, I have a confession to make." He hesitated. "Last night, I spiked your brandy with one of Merlin's love potions."

"That's why you knocked the glass out of my hand?"

"I am sorry, but I thought if you drank the potion and fell in love with me—"

"You believed a magic love potion would work?"

He nodded. "But it did not."

She grinned like a fool—a fool in love. Richard had wanted the magic to work; he had wanted to believe because he *loved* her. Her heart swelled with joy. They didn't need the legend; they didn't need magic.

"I know why it didn't work," she whispered.

"Because Merlin is a fraud."

"No. It didn't work because..." She inhaled deeply to calm herself. "I was already in love with you." He stared at her, his mouth open but no words coming out. She smiled. "I love you, Richard. More than you can possibly imagine.

"The only thing I've ever really wanted was to be loved and accepted. I thought I could find that if I moved out west, but everything I've ever wanted is right here on San Montico. With you.

"Oh, Richard, you've given me more this week than anyone has my entire life. More love, more friendship, more everything. At the press conference, you helped me overcome my fears. As we worked together, you listened to what I had to say. I couldn't ask for anything else. Getting this ring stuck on my finger, meeting you, are the best things that ever happened to me.''

His wide smile, complete with that adorable dimple, crinkled the corners of his eyes. ''Shall we see if the ring is truly enchanted?''

''Do you think...?'' She extended her hand, and he removed her left glove.

Tenderness glimmered in his eyes. As Richard reached for the ring, Christina held her breath with anticipation. He grasped the band. The ring slid from her finger without the slightest hesitation. ''Magic.''

''True love,'' she countered.

''I never believed...until you.''

Richard kissed her, a slow, drawn-out kiss she wished would never end, but when it did Christina realized it was only the beginning, the start of something wonderful, something truly enchanted.

He took a step back and held the ring between his thumb and forefinger. The jewels sparkled beneath the sunlight. ''This belongs to you.''

Legend or not, Richard had chosen her. He loved her, and she loved him. Christina extended her left hand. Richard placed the ring on her finger. A perfect fit.

Epilogue

From the morning edition of the *San Montico Times*...

Royal Wedding Thrills San Montico

The fairy-tale wedding of His Serene Highness Prince Richard de Thierry and Miss Christina Armstrong, daughter of Mr. and Mrs. Alan Armstrong of the United States of America, took place yesterday. Pairs of doves were released into the sky following the nuptial mass. After a procession through the village, a horse-drawn carriage delivered the bride and groom to the palace for a star-studded reception, complete with thirty ice sculptures and a fireworks display.

The bride looked radiant in her silk gown with cathedral train created by local designer, Delia, who has already received international attention and requests for her royal wedding-gown design.

In addition to the stephanotis blossoms and lilies, three white roses were used in the bridal bouquet. The roses, symbolizing the bride, groom and San Montico, were handpicked by Her Serene Highness Princess Marguerite from her award-winning palace garden. The exquisite, pure white bouquet was caught by maid of honor and cousin of the bride, Miss Kelsey Armstrong Waters.

Guests included members of the Aliestle royal family, which marked the first interaction with San Montico in over a century, and the President of the United States and the First Lady, who gave the happy newlyweds a splendid pair of Baccarat candlesticks and a fire extinguisher.

* * * * *

Silhouette ROMANCE™

presents

BRIDAL FEVER!

A brand-new miniseries by
Julianna Morris!

Come to Alaska and meet three
sexy bachelors who have vowed to
never *ever* fall in love.

Watch all three succumb to the three bold and
beautiful brides who capture their hearts!

Available in March 2000:
CALLIE, GET YOUR GROOM

Available in May 2000:
HANNAH GETS A HUSBAND

Available in July 2000:
JODIE'S MAIL-ORDER MAN

Don't miss these delightful stories by Julianna Morris.
Only from **SILHOUETTE ROMANCE®!**

Available at your favorite retail outlet.

Where love comes alive™

If you enjoyed what you just read,
then we've got an offer you can't resist!

Take 2 bestselling
love stories FREE!
Plus get a FREE surprise gift!

MONTANA MAVERICKS
Big Sky Brides

Legendary love comes to Whitehorn, Montana,
once more as beloved authors

Christine Rimmer, Jennifer Greene and Cheryl St.John

present three brand-new stories in this exciting anthology!

Meet the Brennan women:
SUZANNA, DIANA and ISABELLE

Strong-willed beauties who find unexpected
love in these irresistible marriage of
covnenience stories.

Don't miss
MONTANA MAVERICKS: BIG SKY BRIDES
On sale in February 2000,
only from Silhouette Books!

Available at your favorite retail outlet.